Every Day a New Day

and
Other Short Stories

by
Dot Hatfield

Published in Nashville, Tennessee, by Alderson Press.

table of contents

stories

essays

devotionals

Acknowledgements

Every writer who has a book published owes gratitude to a number of people because an effort like this just doesn't come together without the help of friends and family.

First of all, thanks to Steve May, my editor, my son. He was the first to say "publish a book" and then he walked me through the process. Thanks also to Pat Laster, my good friend and writing buddy for the past several years, and to the members of two critique groups, Central Arkansas Writers and First Monday Group. My appreciation goes to all the encouragers in the White County Creative Writers of Searcy, Arkansas.

I appreciate Debbie Oxner, RN, who gave me technical information about pre-natal tests; to M.A., my old friend, for allowing me to use a very real event in his life in the short story "In Our Seventeenth Summer"; and to former co-worker J.H. for loving birds and for letting me watch as she worked her magic.

Thanks to Betty Liddle, my sister, for hours of proofreading and to Phillip Hatfield, my teenager, for providing me with so much essay material over the years.

And finally, thanks to Patsy Pipkin for her kind words.

Dot Hatfield
January 2006

Stories

Every Day A New Day

Roni buried her head deeper into the pillow as Max blew softly in her ear. "Go away!" she moaned. "It's Saturday!"

He persisted. "Come on," he said, tugging at the covers. "Get your sexy body out of bed. We've got lots to do."

She rolled over and stretched. Max was right. She had several things to accomplish before they left on their long awaited, often postponed, second honeymoon.

Last week, they drove to Fort Worth to celebrate their 40th anniversary at a swank restaurant that had a dance floor and a small combo. The first thing Max did after dinner was to ask the bandleader to play "their song," which was experiencing another revival. They glided around the floor just as they did the first time they danced to that tune, as teenagers.

Roni smiled at the remembrance of the romantic evening. Over their last glass of wine, Max pulled out the envelope with the airline tickets to Hawaii. He was so pleased with himself; Roni prayed the trip would be everything they'd dreamed of.

Because when they returned, their children informed them, "a decision would have to be made." After all these years together, her beloved Max was leaving her, bit by bit. The real Max was disappearing; eventually, she would be left with only a shell of what was once a vigorous, funny, intelligent man.

Six months ago, they'd sat together in Doctor Henderson's office, holding hands as they heard his euphemistic phrases: "Short-term memory loss…gradual decrease of sensibilities… increasingly more dependent," until finally, the word was said aloud, sounding the end of their life together.

Since that day, Max had been so reticent about discussing the future, she wondered if he even remembered the conversation.

Roni slid out of bed, found her slippers and put on a robe. She went to the window and looked out. Springtime in North Texas — the loveliest time of year in the most beautiful part of Texas. *Too bad it won't last,* she thought. *In a few weeks, it'll be hot as blazes.*

From their upstairs bedroom, she could see almost a mile across the 320 acres of farmland, where she and Max had come straight from college, carrying their infant son and all of their belongings in their ten-year-old Ford. Max's dad was in poor health and needed him to take over the farm.

Below, in the yard, stood the pecan tree with the tire swing Max had hung almost thirty years ago. Bare spots in the grass underneath it bore evidence of the dragged feet of children and grandchildren. The slope down to the mailbox was covered with primroses. She loved this place. How could she leave?

She could hear Max in the shower and considered joining him as a surprise. She opted for a cup of coffee instead. *I guess we've become old married folks.*

Smiling, she poured water into the coffee maker and thought about their first kitchen — after Max came home from Korea. They had lived in Vet Village, just off the Texas A&M campus. The rows of prefab buildings housed efficiency apartments not much larger than most motel rooms. Their cooking area was so small, she could stand in one spot and reach everything in sight.

Now, she moved about setting plates in the sunny breakfast nook of the old farmhouse, where Max's parents had raised *their* family. Remodeled five years ago, after a tornado picked it up and moved it six inches to the east, the house was as near to perfection as Roni could hope for.

Max came up behind her, breaking into her thoughts. He slipped his arms around her.

"Thank you for last night," he whispered. She turned to give him a kiss.

"You were pretty fantastic yourself."

They held each other a moment and he said into her hair, "I will never forget *this.*"

Every Day a New Day

Roni's breath caught in her throat. Max suddenly broke the mood by slapping her on the behind. She had to laugh at the hug-and-smack routine that had been theirs since the beginning.

"Who's taking us to the airport?" Max asked as they sat sipping refills of coffee.

"Mindy and Joe Don will be here about noon. We have to leave for the airport by five."

"Do you think they want this place?" Max moved his hand in an arc, indicating house and land.

Roni looked into his eyes and saw something bordering on despair.

"No, Max, I don't believe they do. Their lives are pretty centered around their jobs in Dallas."

"What about…" He fumbled with his coffee mug. "…our son?"

"Brad and Susie love bringing the kids here on holidays and summer vacations, but he's been promoted to athletic director at Harlan High, and I don't think they would want to leave Houston right now."

She spoke easily, giving no hint of the conversation she'd had with Brad last week.

"You must realize that you can't live here much longer. You can't take care of things alone."

Brad, their oldest, had no interest in the land where he had grown up. He loved living in the city, coaching football at a large high school. And his wife, Susie, would hate farm life, no doubt about it.

Their daughter, Mindy, had a budding advertising career with a large Dallas agency, and cared so little for the rural life, she rarely visited. Last December, after she and Joe Don moved into their new home, she insisted everyone break with tradition and come to Dallas for Christmas.

Now their children were saying they would have to make a decision. Roni knew it was only a matter of time before she was coerced into moving away from the farm. Several options had been presented and she hated every one of them.

She looked across the table at Max and fought to keep an even tone.

"We don't need to think about that just yet, do we?"

"My grandfather built this house."

"I know, Max."

"I was born in the back bedroom. I planned to die there."

"I know."

"Screw 'em." He pushed back his chair and rose. "I'm going for a ride. Jane and I need the exercise."

"Where are you going? Don't get all sweaty and horsey-smelling."

"Okay. I just need to check some things with Miguel before we leave."

Miguel was more than a hired hand. He had worked for Max for the past fifteen years and would be taking care of the farm while they were in Hawaii.

The thermometer on the barn read 110 degrees the day Miguel came by asking for work. He stayed the rest of that summer to help cut and bale the hay.

The energetic young man had impressed them with his simple lifestyle, sending every spare dime home to Mexico, where the favorable rate of exchange made it possible for his family to survive. When Miguel went home that winter, they didn't expect to see him again. That was the way it was with migrant workers. But he came back the next spring ready for work, and stayed until the hay was baled and the wheat cut.

The third year, Miguel returned and brought Rosita with him. He asked that they be allowed to live in the line shack. Max not only agreed, but also offered Miguel a year-round job.

Within a few months, the shack had been transformed. Miguel repaired the steps, and 'Sita planted flowers around the front door and established a vegetable garden in the back. Over the years, they added a room, hung feed-sack-curtains on the windows, and rigged a pump to bring water into the house. Juan, Bonita and Julio, who had come along in rapid succession, played on their very own tire swing.

Last year, Roni and Max had stood with them in the Federal Court House in Dallas, as Miguel and Rosita Martinez became citizens of the United States.

From the kitchen window, Roni watched Max tighten the cinch

on the mare. He stepped into the stirrup and swung his leg over the saddle. He loved to ride and seldom drove the pick-up unless he needed to carry equipment. How long would he be able to do the simple things he enjoyed so much?

After Max rode out of the yard, Roni worked quickly to check off the items on her list: pay bills, write notes, make calls, stop the mail and the newspaper. She was in the garden looking at her tomato plants when Max returned. He took care of the horse then came out to see her.

"Hi," she said. "Did you have a good ride? How's 'Sita and the kids?"

"Come sit on the porch with me?"

"It's nearly 11:00. The kids will be here soon."

"Okay. Just for a minute?"

They walked to the front of the house and settled into the big rockers that graced the wraparound porch. Roni gently rocked, waiting for Max to say what was on his mind. At last he spoke.

"Our kids had a great time playing on this porch."

"Yes, they did."

"Even when it was raining, they could play outside."

"Yes. That was wonderful."

"I sold Miguel a piece of land."

"You did? What did you sell him?"

"Just what his house sits on...and the north 40 acres."

Roni stopped rocking. She didn't know what to say. Max continued.

"You know, Miguel is a good man. He takes care of things. He's been saving every penny since his mom died, and he stopped sending money to Mexico."

"Yes."

"My dad struggled to keep all this land in our family...but hell, it's the 90's. Maybe it's time for some new blood. Time to give some new Americans a chance at the American Dream."

Tears started in Roni's eyes.

"I called Jerry Dodd. He'll fix the papers and we'll close when we get back."

Roni nodded, unable to speak.

"And Miguel will stay here, Roni. He'll help you when you need it." Max reached for her hand. "I've loved our life on this farm…the memories we have together. The day will come when I won't have them. That's the hardest thing about this…losing our memories."

He brought her hand to his lips and kissed it. She felt a tear touch her wrist. Max took a deep breath and held it for a moment.

"I won't remember the good old days. All I'll have is the present. What can we do about that, Roni?"

"We'll just have to start new memories. Beginning tomorrow morning, when we land in Hawaii, we'll make every day a new day." Roni turned to gaze at the land they both loved.

"Look at the primroses, Max. Their life span is so short…but how spectacular! Life shouldn't be measured by length, but by the beauty it brings to the world."

Linking fingers, they fell silent, each with their own thoughts, accepting this moment of peace as the warm Texas breeze rippled the field of vibrant pink blooms that lined the drive.

~~~

How Long Is Forever

"Are you okay back there, Little Girl?" Aunt Babe called over her shoulder.

"Yes, Ma'am."

"She's so s-w-e-e-t," she said to Granny. Just like I wasn't nine years old and couldn't spell.

The North Texas landscape sped past the car window. It was summer, 1943 — time for baling hay and picking cotton. In the fields, roasting ears stood as tall as me. Hot wind blew my hair. Wiggling a little helped keep my legs off the scratchy upholstery.

I had a secret.

Usually, keeping a secret made me bubbly in my middle. Momma would wonder out loud why all the smiling and ask for clues so she could guess. Finally, my hints would get bigger and she'd figure it out or I would just get too full of the fun and have to tell. But, this was different. My insides felt like dirt instead of bubbles. Part of me wanted to tell, but most of me knew I couldn't.

It should have been a perfect day; at least, that's the way it started. My grandmother and auntie were taking me on a twenty-mile trip over to the next town and none of my little sisters were tagging along. They chose me for this treat as a reward for being a good girl who never caused trouble. I wouldn't spoil the trip by grousing about itchy car seats or July heat.

We left in Aunt Babe's car right after breakfast, with me settled in the back seat sorting my Dionne Quintuplet paper dolls. Aunt Babe and Granny carried on a conversation, raising their voices slightly over the noises of the car motor and the wind. I couldn't hear much of what they said, but that was okay by me. Grown-up talk was either boring or scary. My daddy and uncles always talked about war and politics and the Roosevelts. Woman talk seemed more interesting, if mysterious, with discussions of someone who was expecting because her visitor didn't come. As we rode, I imagined myself as the little English girl who saved Lassie, or Nancy Drew involved in a mystery about an old clock.

At the required wartime speed limit of 35 mph, the drive took the better part of an hour. The morning sun was filtering through the bois d'arc trees when Aunt Babe's car pulled into the long drive leading to the yellow house.

We were taking this trip so Granny and Aunt Babe could check on an elderly relative — a widower who was dependent on the females in the family to come and do for him. From time to time, my grandmother and others would drop by, clean his house, wash his clothes and cook food for him to warm over.

"Bud, this is Charlie and Mary's child. Little Girl, this is your Uncle Bud. Give him a hug, now."

Granny took off her hat and looked around the kitchen, frowning at the breakfast dishes still on the table. I obediently gave Uncle Bud a hug, wrapping my arms around his shaggy neck and allowing him to rub his scratchy cheek on my face. I couldn't remember ever seeing this particular uncle, though his name sounded familiar.

With a family as large as ours, that's not unusual. How he even got to be my uncle isn't clear to me. Probably an in-law. Again, in a big family, it doesn't really matter.

"You're might pretty." He showed a near-toothless grin. "Your name should be 'Pretty Little Girl'." Then he laughed.

He made a joke. Or, he had very bad eyesight. With my straight-as-a-board hair and crooked teeth, I might be called "sweet", sometimes "smart" and often "good", but no one *ever* called me "pretty." The joke wasn't funny, but he was kinfolk and to be polite, I smiled.

"You go find something to amuse yourself, Eula Mae," Aunt Babe said, calling me by my real name. "We'll holler when lunch is ready." I flew out the back door, grateful to be finished with the niceties of talking to old folks.

For the next couple of hours, I explored Uncle Bud's acreage. He

How Long Is Forever

had a garden, which didn't interest me in the least, and an old out building full of various tools. It looked like it might also house rats and other vermin. Finally, a grape arbor on the back of the property captured my attention. The vines nearly touched the ground, bent low with almost-ripe grapes. The space under my ears and jaws crimped at the sour taste.

The arbor had other wonderful possibilities. Betty Grable, in a flowing white strapless evening gown, glided down a long staircase arched with ostrich plumes. Later, a WAC in war-torn Europe, hid from the Germans in a shell of a building. Before I was anywhere near tired of pretending, Granny called from the back door.

The dinner table held my most favorite foods: brown beans, mashed potatoes, fried okra and cornbread. President Roosevelt had asked folks to observe "meatless Tuesdays." My family observed other meatless days, too, eating mostly vegetables from the garden with only an occasional meal that included fried chicken or meat loaf.

After lunch, Uncle Bud challenged me to a game of checkers and showed me the old gramophone in the living room. I had never seen such a thing. A big crank on the side made it go around and the records that fit on the turntable were three times as thick as mine at home. Looking through the stack failed to turn up any familiar songs. One, with a picture of a dog listening to an old-fashioned machine, said "Bing Crosby" on the label. The needle slid into place easily, but the voice that came out sounded high and tinny, nothing like Bing Crosby's deep croon and not nearly as pretty. The old records weren't that much fun after all, so I wandered out to the front porch. Uncle Bud lounged in the swing.

"Hi, Pretty Little Girl. Come over here by me."

Side by side, we sat and talked. In answer to his questions, he learned I was in the fourth grade (when school starts) and yes, I was enjoying summer vacation.

"That's a pretty little dress you have on."

"Thank you."

"Did your momma make that dress?"

"Yes sir."

"What kind of flowers are those on the front there?" He reached over and touched my chest, feeling the flowers on the front of my dress. It felt kind of weird.

"My, my, you are getting to be a big girl, aren't you?" He rubbed the front of my dress again, this time touching the tip of his finger to the end of my tittie that had just that summer begun to grow. This felt more than weird. Actually, in a way, it felt good. My tiny nipple grew hard and a strange ache started somewhere between my legs. In my stomach, the beans and cornbread sat like rocks.

"You have pretty lips, too. Can I kiss you?" Then, before I could answer, he kissed me full on the mouth, just like I had seen in the movies. But, in the movies, it was Rhett Butler and Scarlett O'Hara, not an old uncle with a stubby beard and a scared-to-death little girl.

He kissed me several times. I knew he was kissing me wrong. My mind moved off the porch swing and seemed to be somewhere else, watching what was happening. I saw Uncle Bud put his hand in my lap, touching me between my legs.

I wish Granddaddy was here, I thought.

Why that thought came to my mind just then, who knows? Except — I love my Granddaddy. He knows how old men are supposed to kiss little girls. He would take me on his lap, before I got so big. And I still hug him around the neck and kiss him on the face sometimes. He gives me sugar on the cheek or maybe on the top of the head. Never on the lips. Never like Uncle Bud kept kissing me.

Granny once said Uncle Bud didn't have any children. That seemed sad to me; no children or grandchildren...and he didn't even know the right way to kiss little girls. A huge lump began in my throat and tears rolled from the corners of my eyes. Uncle Bud stopped what he was doing.

"What's wrong, Little Girl?"

"Nothing."

"Why are you crying?"

"I don't know."

He moved away from me suddenly. Something was wrong. I must have done or said something rude — to a grown-up — a relative. More tears welled up and spilled over.

"You don't like me kissing you?"

"Well — sort of — not."

He slid clear to the other end of the swing. This time, there was

How Long Is Forever

no doubt about hurt feelings. I put my hands over my face and sobbed.

"Okay, I'm sorry," he said. "But, I wasn't doing anything. Just don't tell Granny and Aunt Babe. They might get the wrong idea. Stop crying and promise me you won't tell them." He talked real fast. His voice sounded whiney and old. I wiped my eyes with my fists, trying to stop the tears.

"If they found out, you would get in big trouble, you know that, don't you?" His voice sounded stronger and kind of stern.

"Yes, sir, I guess so." I knew no such thing, but I shouldn't dispute a grown-up's word.

"Well, you will. Granny would be so mad at you she would probably cut a switch and give you what for. But, I won't tell if you won't. This can be our secret...promise you won't tell."

"Okay." The tears stopped. What was he saying? I tried to be a good girl. Now he says Granny might get mad at me. How had I gotten into trouble just sitting on this swing?

Aunt Babe came through the screen door taking off her apron. I turned my back to her and dried my face on the skirt of my dress.

"Well, Bud, we got your kitchen squared away. You 'bout ready to go, Little Girl? Tell Uncle Bud you had a nice time."

"I had a nice time."

"Well, you come back soon, you hear?" Uncle Bud patted me on the head. "Thanks, Babe, for the good lunch and all you done."

As Aunt Babe's car puttered toward home, she and Granny chatted about the sorry state of Uncle Bud's affairs: the run-down house, garden full of weeds, no children to look after him.

The North Texas landscape sped past the car window. My head, resting against the glass, filled up with thoughts. How long would I have to keep the secret?

It felt like a long time.

Maybe forever.

~~~

Lost and Found

He looked at his watch as he stepped off the trolley, a half block from the Music Row office building. The digital display showed 2:45. He had plenty of time. *Of all days for the van to mess up. Luckily, she's not working today. She can take the van to the shop.* They had a gig in Asheville, North Carolina, over the weekend and they had to be there. Start canceling dates and your career is over.

Of course, having the van in the shop meant that when Jason called and asked him to come by, he had to take the bus from East Nashville to downtown and catch the trolley to Music Row. A ten-minute trip stretched to twenty.

"Come see me this afternoon." Jason sounded excited. "There's a good chance I can get you a showcase...if you're interested...if you're open to changing the act a little."

If he was interested? Short of appearing on stage naked and playing Musak, there wasn't much he wouldn't be willing to do to jump-start his career. Jason was a good manager; he had brought them a long way and was certainly worth listening to.

****

That stupid van! She had hoped to spend her day off cleaning the house and cooking a great dinner. Instead, she sat in an auto repair shop waiting for an alternator. The thought of driving to North Carolina tomorrow was not appealing, though she was glad for the work. They needed the money. Especially now, with car repairs added to the already strained budget.

When they arrived in Nashville five years ago, with high hopes of breaking into the music business, they quickly found that Music City teems with musicians looking for work. The competition was fierce and the pay low. After two lean years of playing free sets just to be heard, they went on the road.

Writer's Night at the Bluebird Café proved to be a big break for them. Since then, with a manager and a pretty good agent, they often landed dates at resort hotels along the Atlantic coast, mostly on weekends. They were miles ahead of where they had started but still a long way from where *he* wanted them to be.

Part-time, go-nowhere jobs kept food on the table and gas in the van. Home was a rented house in East Nashville, a neighborhood called Historic Edgefield. Some of the houses qualified as historic, but most of them were simply old. Next door sat a beautiful, restored, one-hundred-year-old Victorian, but *they* lived in an ancient house with a leaky roof, bad plumbing and no central heat or air.

She loved it. The spacious yard with the huge trees would make a great place for kids to play. No way children would work into this lifestyle, though. They hadn't even talked about having a baby, but had adopted a yellow cat named Pretty Kitty. P.K. provided company and he took care of himself when they were on the road.

"Your van's ready." The mechanic interrupted her thoughts.

Good. Now, maybe I can get home and get the instruments packed. Then we can rent a movie, order a pizza and relax.

****

As he left Jason's office, the street lights came on, the sensors responding to the darkening sky. *How long was I in there?* He glanced at his watch, then upward. A black cloud hid the April mid-afternoon sun. The air felt heavy and humid as he walked to the bus stop, his head still spinning from the conversation with Jason.

The little change in the act his manager suggested? Go solo.

"Lose her. Her voice is mediocre. Nice, but you could find it behind the counter of any Walgreen's. You're the one with the talent. Lose her, or you'll never go anywhere. Tighten up the act and, in six months, you can be opening for someone like Alan, Shania or Reba. Let me know what you decide."

He sank to the bench, trying to sort out his feelings. *How can I dump her? She's worked hard and sacrificed to help me. But, I didn't beg her to come along. She's here because she wants to be. Maybe Jason's right. Maybe it is time to go it alone. She knows what my music means to me.*

She'll understand. She'll want me to have this chance.

He sighed heavily. His heart and mind knew this to be true. In her completely unselfish way, she would want the best for him.

Suddenly, a barrel blew over, scattering trash as it rolled down the sidewalk. A couple waiting for the bus ran for shelter. A gust of cold air and a spattering of rain brought him to the present. *Maybe I should take cover — that cloud looked menacing.*

As he reached the doorway of a nearby building, he turned to look at the street again. A piece of plywood rose out of a Dumpster and floated away like a feather. Howling wind bent an aged oak tree until it snapped like a twig. Fright gripped him as he watched the funnel cloud descend over downtown Nashville.

****

She knew she must hurry. As the van crossed the bridge over the Cumberland River, the radio announcer urged everyone to take shelter. She needed to get home! She and Pretty Kitty could hide in the basement. The dark and dampness made it less than inviting, but still the safest place in a storm. She parked the van and ran inside calling, "Here, kitty." P.K. was nowhere around. Remembering his favorite hiding place — under their bed — she hurried down the hall. The windows and walls of the old house rattled and groaned.

Stay away from the windows! Find the cat!

The sound of a train bearing down on her was deafening. She dropped on all fours between the bed and the west wall. "Oh, there you are!" she said, just as the locomotive reached the house and the walls collapsed.

****

It took him three hours to get home. Miraculously, the buses were still running, but traffic jams, broken glass and debris in downtown Nashville brought the city to a standstill. The back-up on the Woodland Street Bridge was the last straw. He left the bus and sprinted the rest of the way. After convincing the police officer he lived in the neighborhood, he turned onto Russell Street.

Downtown had been a mess, but what he saw before him was worse. The grand old church — missing its stained glass window.

Fifty-foot trees, heavy with the leaves of late springtime, fallen like Pick-up-Sticks — lying across cars, blocking streets.

In his driveway, the van stood untouched. But their house lay in ruins. A fire truck's rotating light illuminated the scene. Firefighters and volunteers gathered at his house, pulling at boards and shingles, tossing them aside.

The realization of what they might find stopped him short in the middle of the yard. He didn't want to watch but couldn't look away. The thought that she might be lost to him, that he might never again hear her sing, see her smile, touch her hair, brought him to his knees. He tried to formulate some thought, prayer, bargain he could make with God. *Anything* — just to be with her again.

Tears and rain kept him from seeing her when she first crawled through the opening. She stood unsteadily and searched the crowd. He found his voice and called her name. Then she was in his arms. So very much to tell her, but he could only say her name.

After a time, they sat on the wet grass. He cradled her as one would a child, wanting only to keep her near him forever. Pretty Kitty jumped in her lap then, assured all was well, ran off to explore the strange new world.

He held her. His face against her hair, he thought again of the conversation with Jason — a lifetime ago. She would never know. There was no need to tell her. Lose her? His heart tightened and tears stung his eyes at the thought.

****

All around was devastation, yet she was safe. She relaxed, her head against his chest. She heard his rapid heartbeat, felt him shudder with each deep breath. When things were settled, she would tell him. When life was back to normal, they could talk. About her coming off the road. About having a couple of kids. About him going solo for awhile. She hoped he would understand.

<p style="text-align:center">~~~</p>

A Few Minor Adjustments

I lay on my back, feet in stirrups, lights in the delivery room giving a too-white, surreal quality to everything around me.

"It's a girl, just as we suspected," Doctor James said. The nurse hesitated before taking the squealing mass from the doctor's hands.

"Can I see her?" I raised my head, let go of the handles I'd grasped to help push.

"I'll clean her up a bit." The nurse's voice sounded strained behind her mask. She busied herself while the doctor, hidden by the tent of sheets covering my legs, finished suturing. He took my baby from the nurse and brought her to me as I raised my head again to look.

I knew the minute I saw her. The almond eyes, the wide forehead, the chubby cheeks. My daughter had Down syndrome.

My head dropped back on the pillow. Tom, standing beside my shoulder, stepped to my side. He looked white around the lips. Witnessing childbirth had been a little more than he bargained for. He showed no sign that he saw anything unusual about the tiny pink bundle I took from the doctor. Tom kissed the top of my head and gingerly patted the baby's blanket.

I forced a smile. Tired. Time enough to talk later.

* * * *

Oh, the academic discussions we had back in grad school. "If you're going to have a retarded child, Down syndrome is the way to go." This rhetoric, repeated often among fellow therapists during my internship, meant that, while Down syndrome may cause physical problems, there are usually only mild to moderate intellectual impairments. Children with this type of mental retardation can grow up to live satisfactory lives.

We were so objective, so analytical back then. When I was only months away from earning my Music Therapist credentials, feeling the "save the world" enthusiasm, madly in love with Tom and ready to buck my parents and their small-town conventions by moving in with him. We needed no old-fashioned rituals or official papers to prove our commitment to each other.

Of course, in time, I wanted a baby as an expression of our love — to cement our relationship. What is more romantic than to have a baby with your lover? Even if you are more eager for that experience than he.

The routine blood test at fifteen weeks raised questions, but Dr. James reassured me.

"A false positive is not unusual. A sonogram will tell us more."

Sure enough, the more sophisticated test showed I was in my 19th week of pregnancy, almost a month farther along than we thought.

"Aha!" Dr. James smiled. "This could account for a false positive. The baby has a good strong heart beat. Some other things I would like to look at aren't clear, but I'm 90 per cent sure that you have a perfectly normal baby there."

"Ninety percent? Really?"

"Yes. We can do more tests — an amniocentesis — if you want to pursue it."

"No. I feel good. I'm healthy. Ninety per cent is good enough for me."

I was relieved to have it all settled, and glad I hadn't brought Tom into it. Nervous about becoming a dad, he didn't need to worry about tests that turned out to be false. No need to even mention it to him.

* * * *

Sherry, from the residential center where I worked, picked up Tandy and me at the hospital and brought us home. Tom had already moved out.

I stepped into the roomy apartment, stripped now of all that belonged to him, everything that hinted two people had once shared this space. He generously (and probably with some feeling of guilt) left the stereo we had bought together, though most of the CDs were gone. My recliner sat centered in the space that once held two, the dents in the carpet the only evidence of change.

Sherry left, after being assured we were fine, and I sat holding my baby. Tandy stuck two pudgy fingers in her mouth, sucking contentedly. I sang to her softly, "Hush little baby, don't say a word, Papa's gonna buy you..."

The tears came then, as pent up emotion replaced the stoic front I had worked so hard to achieve. *Stop it. You know that crying makes sour breast milk.*

"Well, little Tandy. Looks like it's just you and me. Your Papa has checked out."

I closed my eyes and leaned my head against the chair, trying to organize a to-do list in my head. This exercise usually had a calming effect.

"Let's see. Back to the doctor in four weeks. Check with the day care to see if they take special-needs kids. Make a budget! Can we live if I have to cut back to part time?

Rather than feeling calm, I felt more tense with each item my brain ticked off. I wiped my tears from the top of Tandy's head, curling the soft hair around my finger.

The knock startled me. I lay my baby in her crib and hurried to the door. *Maybe Tom is having second thoughts.*

Mother burst into the room, without waiting to be invited. She brushed past me, pulling the doorknob from my hand.

"Hello, Heather. Your daddy's parking the car." She reached the middle of the room and stopped. Turning, she looked at me. I still stood by the open door.

"Did you plan to tell me about the baby at all?"

I walked back to my chair, leaving the door ajar. "The last conversation we had left me with the impression you were not interested."

"You're my child. Of course I want to know. I had to hear from someone else that... that...there are problems."

"Yes, Mother. Tandy has Down syndrome."

"But...you're young. I thought only older women had...that...sort of baby."

"The odds are against it, but it happens."

"And that man? The baby's father?"

"Color him gone."

"Oh..." Mother sat her purse down on an end table and came to stand by my chair.

"Heather, you just have to look at all of this as God's will. God sent this child to you because you've worked with the handicapped. You know what to say to them and how to treat them. God knew you could take care of a special child. It's a blessing."

"Well, thank you, Loving Heavenly Father!"

"Heather, don't blaspheme."

"I'm sorry. I don't believe that because I choose to go into a low paying job helping others... I volunteer for everything from Save the Whales to Feed the Children. I drive a hybrid. I recycle. Now you say that because I try to be a good citizen, God blessed me with a retarded child."

Mother took a few steps backward before she spoke again.

"The only other logical reason is that it's a curse. It's your punishment for living in sin with that man."

I attempted to leap out of the chair at her, temporarily forgetting what my body had been through the last three days. I wobbled, almost losing my balance. It must have seemed menacing enough, though, because Mother took another step back, bumping into the end table and knocking her purse to the floor. Keys, makeup, and coins spilled out.

"Mother..." I took a deep breath. "My baby has Down Syndrome because a cell divided when it shouldn't have. Look, this is your first grandchild. Possibly your only grandchild. You can shut your mouth and be a part of her life or you can walk out that door. Whichever you do, don't say anything like that to me again. Ever."

We stared across the chasm of silence.

"Hi, girls." Daddy stood at the door. I don't know how much he had heard, but he grinned at me and stepped into the apartment dragging a Bentwood rocker.

"You'll need a rocker," he said.

I went to him and touched the smooth finish of the wood.

"How did you get this in the elevator?"

"With great difficulty." He laughed and opened his arms. He held me a few minutes until I felt some of my tension absorbed by his strength. Releasing me, he said, "Where is she?"

He crossed the room and leaned over the crib. "There she is," he cooed, "there's that little girl. There's my granddaughter." He looked at me and, raising his eyebrows in question, gestured toward my baby. I nodded and he reached down to pick her up.

Mother cleared her throat, reminding us of her presence. "We need…" She stopped and tried again. "May I make some coffee?"

I nodded again and returned to the recliner while Daddy sat in the Bentwood with Tandy, gently rocking. I pulled the lever and leaned back.

Okay, I can do this. Daddy will help me. Mother makes me crazy, but I'll have to deal with that. One of the adjustments I'll have to make. But I can do it. Just a few adjustments.

~~~

Eat Your Heart Out, Doctor Dolittle

"Heeere, birdie, birdie, birdie, birdie, birdie," Nancy chanted as she crept around looking under the table and chairs. We had heard chirping noises the minute we unlocked the door of the Nineteenth Century house that served as offices for our advertising agency.

My name is Andrew Radcliff and my boss, Mr. Aaron, likes for me to get to work promptly at 8:00 a.m. to make sure the thermostat is set at exactly 70 degrees. Usually Nancy, one of the secretaries, is right behind me.

So, as I said, we heard these distressing noises when we first came in and it took us half an hour to figure out the sound came from the parlor that serves as our conference room. In an old house, it is not unusual to have an occasional squirrel in the attic, but a bird in the office was something new.

"I think it's coming from over here." I didn't want Nancy looking under the table and chairs too closely. She might find a few cobwebs and dust bunnies. For the past week, I had been rushing through the nightly cleaning routine in order to get away early and spend more time with the new girl in my life. I couldn't even remember the last time I swept under the table.

Nancy crossed the room to stand by the great sliding door that opened into the hall.

"You think so? I don't...wait a sec..." She cocked her head. "Do you hear that?"

A faint sound came from inside the place where the floor-to-ceiling door slid into the wall. It didn't take much detective work to confirm that indeed a bird hid somewhere inside the opening.

"Oh my gosh! Call 911!" I leapt to obey Nancy's order.

"What's the emergency?" the operator asked.

"There's a bird in the wall!"

Well, I have to admit that the minute those words came out of my mouth I realized how ridiculous it sounded. After I told my name and how I am custodian/handyman/gofer at Aaron Advertising, the operator informed me that a bird in the wall does not constitute a life-threatening situation for a *human being* and furthermore the city prosecutes prank callers.

I hung up the phone and asked Nancy what to do next. We talked it over and decided that if we got out of the way, the bird might leave on its own, but if any of the other employees came along and pushed the solid oak door all the way open, the little one would be killed. The situation was as tenuous as a bumblebee on a cat's nose.

"Hi, Nancy. Hi, Andy. What's happening?" Arizona asked cheerily as she came through the front door. Her waist-length, graying hair, still damp from its daily shampoo, clung to the knitted poncho that provided her protection from the morning chill. Beaded moccasins peeking out from her squaw skirt told us that she rode her bike to work that morning, rather than jogging the three miles from the garage-made-into-an-apartment that she called home.

Our office attire was defined as "dressy casual." Arizona got away with looking like she had made a quantum leap from the sixties because she happened to be the best artist in the business. She didn't find it necessary to see clients and, from the attic office space she shared with her parakeet, she turned out graphics that made huge profits for the company.

Removing the poncho, she revealed a white peasant blouse under a brown-fringed vest, set off by the peace symbol that dangled from a cord around her neck. Before either of us could respond to her greeting, she started for the parlor/conference room.

"Don't open that door!" our voices screeched in unison. She froze in her tracks.

Nancy quickly explained the situation, concluding, "We tried coaxing, but neither of us can communicate with a bird."

"Nothing to it. You just have to know where they're coming from."

She squatted, her thin hips resting on her calves. Peering into the narrow slit where the door receded into the wall, she began making squeaky little noises. We watched as she patiently sat on her haunches and clicked and chirped into the crack. After several minutes, a small sparrow peeked out. Our joy at seeing him erupted into hoorahs of delight and the little head quickly disappeared.

"Cool it." Arizona stood, glared at us briefly, and began her work again.

Twice more, as she talked, the bird crept near. Each time, the ring of the phone or other office noises sent it fluttering back. Finally, trembling, the tiny creature took a few tentative steps out into the room. Moving slowly so her jangling bracelets would not startle it, Arizona took the sparrow in her hands and stepped onto the front porch.

Nancy and I watched as she released the bird and it flew away. We collapsed into chairs, emotionally drained. Arizona waved at the sky and danced back inside, her skirt twirling around her ankles.

"Far out!" Two thumbs, each sporting silver rings, pointed upward.

I took my lunch to the park that day, like always. Finished, I crumbled my bread crust and tossed it on the ground rather than into the Dumpster. Several sparrows flew down from the trees to take advantage of the unexpected repast. I wondered which one of them was free now because a fifty-something hippy spoke his language.

~~~

The Perfect Prize

Rhonda pulled into a parking space in front of Miss Peggy's Playhouse and turned off the motor. She needed to compose herself before picking up Hannah from the day care center. The rambunctious four-year-old would be eager to talk about her day and Rhonda didn't feel up to it just yet. The phone call from Mark right before she left work had upset her more than she would have expected. She wasn't in love with him, she didn't know him well enough for that, but he had seemed like someone who might come to mean something in her life.

His excited voice had made her smile when she heard it.

"Hi, I just got tickets to the Garth Brooks concert tonight; do you want to go?"

"Oh, gee, I can't. I — I have something."

"Well, I know it's last minute, but these are great tickets. It's his farewell tour. You can't get out of it?"

"No, it's my night with Hannah."

"Hannah!"

"Yes, I reserve Thursday night for Hannah. I never do meetings or anything else on Thursday. Even if the rest of the week gets crazy, she can count on that special time."

"Can't you explain to her that this is a once in a lifetime deal?"

"She's four years old. She wouldn't understand. We always have Thursday night together"

"I can't believe you're giving up the opportunity to see Garth Brooks to spend the evening…" He stopped without finishing the sentence. He sounded angry.

Rhonda took a deep breath, feeling herself bristle at the irritation in his voice. She tried to think of something to say that wouldn't blow this into a full scale fight. He spoke first.

"Okay. Have a nice evening. I'll call you."

Rhonda hung up the phone with finality. *So much for Mark. I'll never hear from* him *again.*

She could deal with the fact that he would dump her over this. In fact, the routine was becoming old hat. Men seemed to avoid a relationship with her because of her daughter. One expressed the opinion that Hannah took too much of her time. Another said his life was complete without the "complication" of a child. And at least two others had said, "I'll call you" and just didn't.

Getting pregnant right out of high school and having her marriage fall apart had forced Rhonda to mature early. At twenty, she had found herself single with a toddler to support. She worked hard to complete a computer course and find a decent job. When she began to date again, she realized from the beginning that if she didn't set firm priorities, Hannah would be neglected. Rhonda knew she had made the right decision.

She rang the bell on Miss Peggy's front door, looking forward to a big hug from Hannah, which never failed to brighten her day. Twenty minutes later, the two sat on the playground of Hannah's favorite eating place. The little girl chatted happily while she squeezed catsup from the packet onto her fries. Suddenly, she squealed with delight. "Look! There's Allison! She goes to my school!"

Rhonda turned to see a little girl about Hannah's age sitting at a table near the jungle gym. The child waved frantically. The familiar-looking blond man sitting with her smiled and raised his hand in half salute.

Daddy's visitation. Rhonda nodded in return.

"Can I go say 'hi' to Allison?"

"All right, for just a minute."

The two walked across the playground. Before either parent could say a word, the children giggled, "Let's crawl through the tunnel," and ran off to play.

"It seems our girls have plans of their own," the blond man said. "Would you like to sit down?"

"Sure, thanks. This is Hannah's absolute favorite place to eat. I could never decide if the fascination was the prize in the Junior Meal or the playground. Now, I'm sure the chance to see Allison will add to the attraction."

The man smiled. "I'm Rusty Colby, otherwise known as 'Allison's Daddy'."

Rhonda introduced herself and they fell into an easy conversation about the pros and cons of fast food restaurants, day care in general and Miss Peggy's Playhouse in particular. She felt comfortable with him; they seemed to share the same quirky sense of humor, which pleased her. As they talked, Rhonda realized how involved Rusty stayed in Allison's life. She admired him for that, knowing how difficult it could be for the non-custodial parent.

"I'm sorry to break this off," Rusty said finally, "But I promised to take Allison to see her grandmother." He raised his voice slightly and called, "Allison, time to go."

The two little girls came running to their parents, laughing. Rusty bent to tie Allison's shoe. With surprise, Rhonda realized they had been talking for over an hour. During their exchange she had completely forgotten the earlier confrontation with Mark.

"I've enjoyed talking to you tonight," Rusty said as he set Allison on the ground. "I don't have many opportunities for adult conversation." He looked at Rhonda and continued. "I would like to call you sometime, but I need to say up front that I am a full time parent. Allison gets most of my time and attention."

Rhonda busied herself with gathering up the remains of their meal. *He seems nice enough, but, do I want to try again?*

When she didn't speak, Rusty shrugged slightly and smiled.

"Maybe we'll see you and Hannah here again sometime. Tell your friend bye-bye, Allison."

Rhonda watched the pair leave the playground, then sank to the bench. *Well, I blew it. He's an interesting and likable man who would surely understand about Hannah. Why didn't I say something? Am I afraid?*

"Will you help me open my toy?" Hannah pulled on her mother's sleeve, handing her the plastic bag that held the prize from her meal. Rhonda absent-mindedly pushed her nail through the bag and removed the toy. She automatically checked it for loose parts.

The small globe filled with liquid held a cartoon character inside. When she shook it, one or two pieces of glitter floated languidly around the scene. She handed the prize to her child.

"Do you like this toy, Hannah?" The four-year-old looked it over.

"It's not so good. But that's okay. I still like to come here 'cause when you open the box you never know 'zactly what the prize will be. Sometimes it's not so good, but sometimes it's *perfeck*. You just take your chances."

Sure you do. Whether it's Junior Meal toys or relationships, you must be willing to take your chances. Too bad I let this one slip by. It might have been perfect.

Rusty's voice broke into her thoughts.

"Allison forgot her toy, is it here?"

Startled, Rhonda jumped up and helped Rusty look for the plastic bag from Allison's meal. She spied it under the table, retrieved it and handed it to him. He turned the prize over in his hand.

"It's not much, is it?"

"Not this time." Rhonda smiled. "But sometimes they're wonderful. You just take your chances...uh...just a minute..."

She fished in her purse for a pen, found an almost-clean napkin on the table and scribbled down her phone number. Folding the napkin, she handed it to Rusty.

"In fact, sometimes the prize is *perfeck*."

~~~

Consider the Bluebonnets

February 17, 1862 Fannin County, Texas
My dearest husband,

I take pen in hand to write on the seventeenth day of February, the year of our Lord 1862. Today I walked to the south pasture and sat for awhile under the bois d'arc tree where our son lies. The carving stating his name has weathered well through the winter. Papa says one day he will bring a stone to mark the spot forever. Feeling new life move inside my body eases the grief over the loss of little Jerome Leonidas, Junior, who died even before he could be baptized.

Dr. Penray says walking is good for me, but Mother Coker worries the pasture is far from the house and there is still a chill in the air. So I will not go again until I can take our new child with me. Just a few more months. I pray that by then you will be safely home with us. Lee, I miss you so.

You said pencil and paper is hard to come by, so I will not mark on the back of this letter. Use that space to answer and when Mose Atkins delivers supplies to your camp I will send tablet and pencil. I remain your loving wife, Jane Coker.

MJ Coker to JL Coker, 34th Cavalry, Somewhere in Arkansas

March 15, 1862 Camp Caudle, Benton County, Arkansas
Dear Companion,

Your letter of February 17 warmed my heart. I am sorry to be far from you at this time. I pray God will watch over you and keep you safe. I do not understand this war. I see no sense in secession nor rebellion. You know I voted with the majority of Fannin County against it, though our state as a whole agreed to stand with the South. That being done, I must be loyal to Texas. The irony is that we Cokers do not own slaves. The whole family together could not raise enough money for one good black. It just makes me wonder why I fight a war I don't believe in. But better here than on the frontier fighting Indians.

Us boys from Caney Creek try to watch out for each other. Because we are farmers and don't have much fighting skills, the regular soldiers think less of us. Since we brought our saddle horses from home, we are called the "Plow Horse Cavalry."

There is sickness in camp. Several of the boys in our brigade are ailing, but God has blessed me with good health. I pine for you and home. Tell Papa to get Thom Curtis and see to my new calves if they can. Your husband, J. Leonidas Coker

JL Coker to MJ Coker, Caney Creek, Fannin County, Texas.

April 10, 1862 Fannin County, Texas
My dearest husband Lee,

I received your letter and am so thankful to hear you are well and safe in body, though low in spirits. We are all in good health here. Your father had a spring cold but is fairing well now. He and Thom Curtis have branded six fine calves for you. One cow got down and couldn't get up so they had to destroy it. However, another cow took her calf, so all is well there. The fields are beautiful and green. The cattle should have plenty of grass this summer when the heat comes.

I am feeling well, though very heavy with our child. The front porch you put on the house last year is such a blessing. I sit there and sew and enjoy the warm sun and see the patches of bluebonnets that dot the field on the way down to the road. I imagine one day sitting and watching children at play. The children I pray God will give us. Today, as I considered the bluebonnets, a scripture came to mind. *"Consider the lilies of the field. They toil not, neither do they spin. But even Solomon in all his glory was not arrayed like one of these."* I thought to myself, no fine lady in the North, even Mrs. Lincoln herself, has such a view from her front porch!

Please keep safe, my love, as you fight battles in places I barely heard of before this awful war invaded our lives. Take heart that as much as my love is for you, God's love is greater. I pray he will keep you safe. My truest love to my husband, your wife, Jane Coker.

MJ Coker to JL Coker, 34th Texas Cavalry in Arkansas

May 1, 1862 Pea Ridge, Arkansas
Dearest Companion,

Your letter came to hand last week but we were on order to move the next day to this spot. This was the site of a battle last year where each side lost over 1,000 men. From here, it is my guess we will scout over into Missouri. Thank you for the clothes and the paper for writing. My boots were near worn out for sure.

How I wish I could be with you in beautiful Texas springtime. The weather here has warmed but is still cold at night. It was a hard winter to be in camp and some of the boys are still sick. A few were left behind in homes where they can have care and sleep warm. They will join us later if God wills and they get well. We have seen few battles and it looks like typhoid will kill more of us than the Feds ever do. All the while, our women folk do the best they can at home without us, and our crops and cattle go untended. You are the brave one, my love.

Forgive me, Janey, for having no good cheer. Soon your time will come and I pray for a healthy new son for us. I also pray for courage for you and that our Lord will be with you when I cannot. I am the same in love as I ever was. Leonidas Coker.

JL Coker to MJ Coker, Fannin County, Texas

May 15, 1862 Fannin County, Texas
Dearest Son,

I take my pen in hand to write that your wife Jane gave birth to a fine son on Monday this week. He is healthy, with good color and a strong cry. It was a long hard travail for Jane. She was very weak when it was over and had lost much blood. It grieves me to tell you she did not live but only 8 hours. She kissed your child and then she passed on to be with our Lord. She named your son Americus Leonidas. Papa and the men of the church buried Jane under the bois d'arc tree near your first son. She loved that spot and visited it often. Today it was full to glory with the bluebonnets she took such fondness for. The circuit rider will be here next week and hold a service. He will baptize the baby, as this was the last thing Jane asked.

My heart grieves for your loss and my own. I loved Jane as a daughter. Be assured every member of the family pledges to care for your child with love and tenderness till you are home.

Two of your cows are fresh so there is plenty milk for the baby and the whole family. Little Lee has taken to the cow's milk very well. You are always in my prayers for God to keep you safe and bring you home to your son. Your loving mother, Mary Elizabeth Coker.

ME Coker to JL Coker, 34th Texas Cavalry, Arkansas

June 1, 1862 Pea Ridge, Arkansas
To Mrs. Mary Elizabeth Coker and family.

It is with greatest sympathy I take my pen this day to inform you of the death of your son, Jerome Leonidas Coker, Private, 34th Texas Cavalry. Private Coker was on scout to Missouri and camped near Elk River when he was snake bit. We have since learned snakes are very bad in that area. The snake got in his bedroll and Pvt. Coker was bitten in the back. There was little we could do for him but try to keep him easy. In his last hours, he spoke of love for his family and concern for his new son.

Mr. Mose Atkins will be returning to Fannin County tomorrow after delivering supplies. He will bring Pvt. Coker's body back to Texas, arriving one week hence. Your son's last request was that he be buried in the field of bluebonnets next to his wife and son.

Please convey my sincere sympathy to all Pvt. Coker's kin and know that even though he did not die in battle, he gave his life as a brave soldier for the Confederate States of America. My deepest regards, Lt. Daniel J. Merrick, 34th Texas Cavalry, CSA

Lt. DJ Merrick to Mrs. ME Coker, Fannin County, Texas

~~~

When There's Nothing to Do

Sarah slammed her fist against the steering wheel as the cars in front of her slowed to a stop. For the past hour, a wreck on Interstate 40 had caused traffic to creep along in the 90-degree heat. She glanced at her watch as she pulled off Exit 12 in Memphis. 7:00 p.m. already! She would spend the night here.

After Joy's call about their dad, Sarah had left Nashville right after lunch, planning to stay over in Little Rock. From there, the drive to Dallas was easy. Now with these delays, rather than arriving tomorrow in the early afternoon, she would be fighting rush hour traffic.

Sarah dropped her bag in the motel room and sat on the edge of the bed. Why was she making the twelve-hour trip to see her dad? Their time together was always spent laughing and joking or having a dinner of Dad's favorite chicken-fried steak. Would the joy still be there? Or would future uncertainties cast a cloud?

With a sigh, she let her body fall back across the bed and she lay there, staring at the ceiling. She thought again of her sister's words, "Congestive heart failure…maybe six more months…down hill all the way from here." Sarah tried to rationalize; *Dad's 80 years old. He's had a good life. But, he's Dad! He's still bright and wise and useful. Whatever will I do without him?*

"I'm coming," Sarah told her sister.

"Fine, come on," Joy's voice sounded flat. "But there's nothing you can do here."

Nothing she could do? She was Managing Partner of a major investment firm. She took charge of complicated situations every day. Through hard work, she had established herself in a highly competitive business. She was at the peak of her earning power, fully vested in a comfortable retirement plan. Nothing she could *do?* She shut her eyes tightly to hold back the threatening tears. "Stop it," she said out loud. She rose quickly, deciding to go for a swim before supper.

On top of her swimsuit lay the Bible Dad had given her for Christmas nearly twenty years ago. She had hurriedly tossed it in the suitcase just before fastening the lid. Now, she picked it up. Tucked between the pages was the daily Bible reading guide she followed occasionally. Her hectic life did not allow time to read every day. She opened the book. Maybe there would be some answers in the scriptures.

Slowly, Sarah read from Mark 14: the story of the woman from Bethany who anointed Jesus with perfume. The disciples scolded the woman for being so wasteful, but Jesus understood her gift, saying, *"She has done a beautiful thing to me...You will not always have me. She did what she could...to prepare my body for burial. ...wherever the gospel is preached, what she has done will also be told..."*

As she read, tears filled her eyes and dropped on the pages, blurring the words. *"...She did what she could...prepare my body for burial. You will not always have me."* Sarah had hoped for comfort. Instead, the words seemed to accent her grief.

She shut the book. "I will not cry," she said, snatching her swimsuit from the bag. "I need a swim."

Sarah was glad to find the pool almost deserted. A man sat in the lounge chair, fully clothed, obviously not planning to swim. A woman wearing a floppy hat gave him a wave as she walked through the gate of the pool area. Sarah sank into a nearby chair, twisting her hair into a knot and fastening it with a clip.

"She wanted to come to Memphis to see Graceland," the man said. Sarah looked up. There was no one else the man could be talking to, so Sarah asked politely if they had enjoyed the tour of Elvis' home.

"I don't care much about that sort of thing, but she wanted to come. So, we came over yesterday and went to Graceland today." He gazed at the woman as she walked to the edge of the pool and bent to test the water.

"She has a doctor's appointment in Nashville tomorrow, but she wanted to come to Memphis first."

Sarah did not want to seem rude, but was not sure why he was telling her this.

The woman walked to the chair beside the man, took off her robe and kicked out of her sandals. She removed the hat. With one look, Sarah knew the reason for the trip to Nashville. The wispy tufts of hair, either falling out or growing in, the evidence of the aftermath of chemotherapy, explained it all.

The woman lowered herself into the pool and floated on her back. She closed her eyes, completely relaxed, a faint smile playing around the corners of her mouth. Sarah watched the woman move in the water, unable to look away from the expression of pure enjoyment.

While his wife swam, the man told Sarah they were to see a doctor at Vanderbilt Medical Center to talk about the possibility of a bone marrow transplant. Sarah murmured some reply about the doctors at Vanderbilt being wondrously wise and assured the man his wife would have the best of care.

But, Sarah was thinking of 1981: Dad and Mother making the weekly trips to Dallas for the treatments that left Mother nauseated and weak. Dad would find a new restaurant to try, a movie they had never seen, or something special to do to make the day seem lighter. He still loved to tell about seeing "*On Golden Pond*," featuring two favorite actors, now seniors also. They sat in the theater holding hands, thinking of the Hepburn and Fonda of their courting days.

Mother always went along with Dad's plans, enjoying the sights, smells, and sounds of each experience while it lasted. Dad relished these outings he planned for them together. It was something he could do for her.

The woman climbed out of the pool and toweled herself dry as she and her husband carried on an animated conversation about where they should have dinner. Sarah watched as they walked through the gate, hand in hand, laughing softly.

She leaned back in the lounge chair. As the last rays of sun reflected off the pool, she said a silent prayer for the man and his wife. She added a thank you for her parents and the love they had

shared. She thought again of the woman from Bethany, showing
Jesus her love in the best way she knew how. *"She did what she could."*

Sarah had her answer. What do you do when there's nothing to
do? You do what you can. You show your love: lavishly, as the
woman from Bethany, or simply, as Dad and the man at the pool.
You give a lovely gift, you see a movie, you go to Graceland, you take
your dad out for chicken-fried steak.

~~~

When There's Nothing To Do

Called To Be A Dad

Joseph filled his cup to the brim with the red liquid from the wineskin then, without taking a sip, he pushed it away. He welcomed the warm feeling he knew the drink would bring to his body and he longed for the dulling effect it would have on the pain in his heart. Still, he could not afford that luxury right now. He needed to keep his senses sharp. He must think and make some clear decisions.

Just a few hours ago Mary, the young girl he had come to love, the one he had chosen to be his wife, stood before him and told him the most outrageous story he had ever heard.

"Joseph, I don't know how to say this. I can only pray you will understand and hope that God has given you a sign, too."

And then she told him she was with child. She swore she had not lain with another man, however. She said an angel had told her that the babe she carried was the long-expected Messiah …the one Prophesy said would come to Israel to save the people from their enemies.

After Mary finished speaking, Joseph could not respond. It was as though he had been struck dumb. Not only had this girl betrayed him with another man, she now blasphemed God with this preposterous claim! If the townspeople did not stone her for the first offense, they would certainly do so for the second.

After several minutes of silence, Mary said, "I know you find this impossible to believe, but it is true." Without another word, she turned and walked out of the carpenter's shop, taking his hopes and dreams for the future with her.

Darkness had gathered around Joseph, so he lit the lamp. A

sense of habit rather than hunger directed him as he broke off a piece of the loaf and cut a slice of cheese for his supper.

Maybe Mary was mistaken…many virgins came to the marriage bed with no understanding of what it took to make babies. At any rate, if she was pregnant, some man must have taken advantage of her. Try as he might, Joseph could not bring himself to believe that Mary was a wicked, blasphemous girl trying to use the belief in the Promised One to cover her own sins. There had to be another explanation.

She had taken leave of her senses. An evil spirit had come to possess her, making her insane. He would talk to her father tomorrow. They would devise a plan to put her away safely. Joseph could not bear the thought of her being branded a harlot…or worse. He shuddered at the image of her delicate form being stoned in the market place…which would surely happen if her sin was discovered and she told her wild tale about angels.

Joseph wrapped his robe around him and lay down on his mat. Perhaps God meant for him to live and die without a wife to warm his hearth or a child to carry on his name.

"Oh, Lord," he cried in his grief. "Show me what to do. Give me a sign."

* * *

"Joseph, son of David."

The voice spoke to him while he slept. Aware that he was still lying on his bed, within his dream Joseph saw the man standing before him. A light brighter than one could even imagine radiated from the stranger who Joseph realized must be an angel.

"Joseph, son of David. Do not be afraid to take Mary as your wife, because what is conceived in her is from the Holy Spirit. Mary will give birth to a son and you are to give him the name Jesus, because he will save his people from their sins. You will have no union with her until after the child is born."

Suddenly, the dream ended. Joseph sat straight up on his bed. The room was dark as the inside of a cave.

Could this be true? Had God sent the messenger in answer to his prayer? Was his Mary chosen by God to be the mother of the

Promised One? He lay back on the mat, his eyes open to the utter blackness around him. He thought of Mary and their conversation earlier. His heart filled with love for her and shame that he had needed the angel to confirm what she had told him. He should have had enough respect and love for her to believe her without any other proof.

Joseph rose and walked through the curtain that led from his house into his work area. The moon in its last quarter cast a dim light through the door of the shop. He moved his hand across the smooth wood of the table he was working on when Mary interrupted him. He thought, *I will need to make a cradle.*

Stepping into the courtyard, he gazed into the heavens at the bright stars shining on the sleeping village. He fell on his knees.

"God of Abraham, Isaac and Jacob. Here am I, your servant. You have called Mary to be the mother of a child conceived by the Holy Spirit. You have called me to be her husband. I do not understand how all this can be, but I know that with you all things are possible."

So Joseph took Mary as his wife. Some of the old wives in town counted on their fingers and gossiped that Joseph had acted irresponsibly…had been too eager to wait patiently for his wedding night. Either that or he had been made the fool by this young girl who looked so innocent.

Joseph paid them no mind. He vowed to shelter Mary from any hurt that might come from such busybodies. The angel had told Joseph not to take Mary as his wife until after the child's birth. Not an easy thing to do. The quest of every Jewish man was to produce sons to carry on his heritage, just as the duty of a Jewish wife was to please her husband in every way. But their special circumstances allowed Mary and Joseph to have a very different relationship… one based not on sexual pleasure or the desire for children but grounded in a common task God had given each of them to do. As the months went by, Joseph's love for Mary grew deeper than he had ever believed possible.

And then, when Mary was great with child, they had to travel to Bethlehem. Joseph delivered the baby there in the barn, awestruck as all young fathers are at the miracle of birth. He cleaned the child, wrapped him in cloths and put him in Mary's arms.

As she held the baby to her breast, Joseph gently kissed the woman he loved so dearly. He stepped out of the stable into the cool winter night.

Again, as on the night of the angel's visit, he looked at the heavens. One star seemed particularly bright in the black sky. Joseph raised a prayer of thanksgiving. He vowed to be true to the role God had given him, to be a good father to this child, and to always, always trust God even when the situation seemed impossible.

~~~

The Substitute Boy

"No, we won't try again. No point in filling up the yard with girls, trying to have a boy."

From my favorite hiding place, I could hear the voices from the nearby park bench.

I didn't know the women sitting on the bench, though I could guess that the one speaking must be the mom of the three little red-headed girls in the sandbox near the swings. It could have been my own mother talking.

Behind the bench nearest the playground, where moms rest and watch their kids climb on the monkey bars, a thick juniper separates the park from a storage building where the city keeps lawn equipment. The hedge bends low in front but is hollowed out in back. Anyone sitting in the reamed out space is well hidden.

Since finding the spot over three years ago during a game of hide and seek, I came often. Sometimes, just to be alone with my own thoughts. At nine-going-on-ten, I was almost too big to fit under the bush but I didn't want to think about looking for another place.

My oldest sister, Janet, turned fifteen this year. Sharon is three years younger. Then comes me, Jimmie. My dad's name is James. The message couldn't be clearer if I wore a sign: "We tried, we failed, we gave up. This is our substitute boy."

As each of us reached the age of five, our world expanded. Janet enrolled in dance classes and Sharon studied piano. I played T-ball. By the time I started to school, I had a closet full of sports equipment. Soft ball, soccer and basket ball...as soon as one season ended, practice for the next sport began.

So, there I sat on a Tuesday afternoon, trying to build up my courage to face Dad. It was the first week in May, so instead of practice, we scrimmaged with another Little League team. Dad was working and couldn't be there, but he would want a full report at supper.

I struck out…on a called third strike. One of Dad's cardinal rules is: go down swinging. Don't stand there with the bat on your shoulder and let the ump call you out.

Then, playing short stop in the third inning, I bent to pick up a grounder just as it took a hop over my head. I'm not sure what I did wrong there, but Dad would know and after supper, he would knock grounders to me until dark. Even though Mrs. Davis, the scorekeeper, said, "Hey, Jimmie, that ball took a bad hop. It was a hit, not an error," that wouldn't matter to Dad. He liked for me to steal someone's hit by snagging an impossible ball. We practiced a lot because he wanted to help me be the best player possible.

I realized I had been sitting way too long, so I crawled down the hedgerow, staying close to the building until I reached the corner. I stood and walked out from behind the bushes and started back toward the ball field.

"Jimmie."

I stopped at the sound of my mother's voice. She and my sisters stood at the edge of the parking lot near our van. As I reached them, Janet said, "What were you doing in those bushes?"

"I know," Sharon butted in.

"Nothing," I answered quickly. *Oh, shoot. Sharon must know about my hiding place. Think fast!* "Looking for a tennis ball I lost Saturday."

"No you weren't," Sharon sing-songed.

"Jimmie, were you peeing in there?" Janet always acted like someone put her in charge of my behavior.

"No! MOM?"

"Okay, girls, that's enough. Get in the van. We're going to pick up something for supper. What'll it be?"

I climbed into the backseat of the Caravan as far from my sisters as possible. Janet had called shotgun for the rest of her life and Sharon had her homework spread all over the middle seat. I didn't care. The back suited me fine…away from Janet's bossiness and

Sharon's long nose.

Mom turned onto Diane Brady's street. Diane was in Janet's ballet class. Mom gave her a lift to the studio every Tuesday and Thursday and in return Mr. or Mrs. Brady delivered Janet to our house when class was over. That way, we could go home and start supper and Janet would eat when she got in.

As we stopped at Diane's house, Mom asked again what we would like to eat. It didn't matter to me, but I said, "Chinese" just to start a discussion. Sharon hated Chinese.

Tuesday was a free day for Sharon. She had piano on Monday and Thursday, Pep Squad on Wednesday and band on Friday. Every Tuesday, during my softball practice and Janet's dance stuff, she did homework. Then, when we got home, she could do whatever she wanted. Janet and I followed the same routine on our free days.

Mom let Janet and Diane off at the studio and we headed home. I saw Dad's car in the driveway when we pulled in. My stomach knotted as I gathered up my bat and glove, expecting his sure-to-come questions about the game this afternoon.

He kissed Mom and Sharon and tousled my short shag cut.

"Hi, Jim. How'd we do today?"

"We won, 10-3."

"Great! How'd *you* come out?"

"I went two-for-three."

"Two for three! What happened?"

"Bad eye, I guess."

"You watched a strike go by?"

"I guess so."

Dad started to say more, but Mom cleared her throat and he seemed to change his mind.

"Okay, no problem. We'll do some batting practice after supper."

Mom set the table and put out the variety of Chinese dishes, with a plate of American fried chicken for Sharon. She covered Janet's plate and put it in the refrigerator to microwave later.

Maybe Sharon was doing homework during the game and didn't see the bobbled grounder. If she'll just keep her mouth shut...

Mom filled our plates and sat down across from Dad.

"James, tomorrow after you pick up Sharon from pep squad, can you stop by the park and get Jimmie? I need to take Janet to church by 4:30 for youth choir practice."

"I'm not sure Janet should get into any more activities. Wednesday is supposed to be her free day."

"When she can do what she wants..." Mom's voice trailed off as she took a sip of her tea.

 I chomped down on an egg roll, then remembered the invitation.

"Mom, Friday is Angie Branch's birthday. She's having a sleep-over. Can I go?"

"Well, how nice. I don't see why not..." She glanced at the calendar on the refrigerator. "Oh..."

"What?"

"There's the softball tournament on Saturday."

"That's Saturday. The party is Friday...my free day."

"I know, but the games start early. Your team plays at 8:30." Mom looked at Dad, who spoke up.

"I don't think so, Jimbo. You'll be too tired to play if you stay up all night giggling with a bunch of girls."

"I won't. I promise I'll go to bed early and get plenty of rest." I looked from one to the other. "Do I have to go to the tournament? I missed the movie party because of soccer." When they didn't say anything, I knew the answer. "It's not fair..." This was the whiniest thing I could possibly say, but I couldn't help myself. Dad dropped his piece of chicken in his plate.

"We've had this conversation before. They're counting on you and it wouldn't be right to let them down."

I knew Dad was telling the truth. But a sleep-over!

For once, Sharon kept her nose in her plate and her mouth shut. The egg roll lodged halfway down the middle of my chest.

"May I be excused?" I hoped I could make it to the bathroom in time.

"Okay," Dad said. "Start your homework. We'll skip batting practice."

"Thank you." I scooted out of the dining room and upstairs before he changed his mind.

As I reached the top of the stairs and passed Janet's room, I stopped. There, on her closet door, hung the most beautiful sight I

The Substitute Boy

had ever seen. Yards and yards of lavender tulle attached to a matching bodice with little spaghetti straps holding it on the padded hanger. Janet's costume for her spring dance recital. She and two other girls would be performing a dance from Swan Lake.

This was a big step up from last winter's production of The Nutcracker, when she played the third flower on the left. She had auditioned for a solo and we were all disappointed for her when she didn't get it. Dad decided she should take an extra day of dance this summer, to improve her chance of getting a big part next year — maybe even the Sugar Plum Fairy — if she didn't have some sort of weird growing spurt before then. She already watched her carbs, since ballerinas can't carry extra weight and still perform well.

I forgot about the urge to throw up. Carefully removing the tutu from the hanger, I held it in front of me and looked in the full-length mirror. Without stopping to think, I shut the bedroom door, peeled off my shirt, lifted the filmy material and let it fall around my body.

The outfit was a little large for me, the straps fell off my shoulders and the stretchy top didn't cling to my skinny rib cage as tight as it should, but it felt luscious. Rising on tiptoe, I held my arms out and tried to twirl as I had seen Janet do. I didn't hear the door open.

"What are you doing?" Janet stood there, dance bag in one hand and her back pack in the other. Either one could deal a fatal blow if applied up side my head. Fortunately, she opened her hands and let them both drop to the floor. She headed toward me.

Already wiggling out of the tutu, my thumbs hooked in the bodice, inching it down past my hips, I stepped wide over the mound of tulle to avoid smashing the skirt.

"Wait a minute," I said to my advancing sister. I grabbed the tutu and put it back on the hanger, a little crooked but off my body and off the floor...good as new. Janet kept walking until she came close enough to touch me.

"Were you trying on my dance costume?"

"Yes...but...I just wanted to see it. I didn't hurt it."

"Why would *you* want to put on a tutu?" Her eyes narrowed. "Are you trying to be a girl?"

Tears started. I could hardly speak around the lump in my throat.

"I *am* a girl, Janet."

She reached toward me and I flinched, sure she was going to give me such a smack. But, instead, she took my arm and led me over to her bed.

For I-don't-know-how-long, we sat cross-legged in the middle of her ballerina bedspread and talked. We talked about dancing and softball and a million other things. It felt wonderful. After awhile, we agreed we'd better get to our homework. But, as I stood up, Janet grabbed my hand and said, "Come on." She led me downstairs to the den.

Dad sat in his recliner reading the newspaper while Mom folded a basket of laundry. Sharon held her Gameboy, her thumbs manipulating the buttons. Janet raised her voice to get their attention.

"Mom and Dad. Jimmie wants to take dance and I want to go out for cheerleader."

All three glanced up and several seconds went by without anyone saying a word. Then, as one, my parents turned toward Sharon.

"I'm good," she said, going back to her game. This seemed to jar Dad into speech.

"Now, Janet, about cheerleading. You know that with all those tumbles and jumps and pyramids there's a danger of your injuring an ankle. What would that do to your chances to dance Sugar Plum Fairy or Snow Queen?"

"I don't want to be Snow Queen…Jimmie wants to be Snow Queen."

"Jimbo? Dance?" He sounded as though he might be trying to understand an unknown language. His hand covered his mouth…maybe to hide a smile. I found my voice.

"Or Clara, or a tin soldier or even a mouse."

"What about softball?"

I felt myself hesitate, but Janet spoke up.

"Jimmie wants to quit Little League and join the church team. Only one practice and one game a week, never on Wednesday or Sunday."

"That would be nice," Mom said, almost under her breath.

Dad raised his eyebrows, about to say something to Mom, but he turned back to me.

"Jim, if you drop out and give up your spot on the roster, you might not get it back."

"That would be okay with me."

"Okay with *you*!" The vein on his temple was clearly visible. I had seen it before, but not often.

Well, softball and dancing were discussed thoroughly for the next hour. No one said anything new; we repeated ourselves often. Then finally, just like the cowardly lion, and with Janet for support, I got me some nerve. I spoke up bravely.

"Okay. I'll play Little League…if I can dance, too." After that, we arrived at some compromises.

Janet can try out for cheerleader and if she makes it, she won't take summer dance classes. Instead, she'll drop her tap class to take the extra ballet lesson. On Wednesday, while I have baseball, Mom will drop Janet off at church so she can sing in the youth choir.

I'll play Little League this summer and start dance in September instead of playing soccer. We'll talk about the church league next year when it's time to sign up for softball again.

"Maybe golf's a better sport for you anyway," Dad said.

Everyone froze like they do in that commercial and waited to see if we were going to go another round.

"Sure," I said. "Sounds like fun."

Mom exhaled, Janet rolled her eyes and looked at the ceiling and Sharon raised her Gameboy a little closer to her face, her thumbs moving wildly.

But, it really *is* okay with me…because guess what?

Friday night, I'm going to my very first sleep-over.

~~~

An Answer to Prayer

Clay sat in his car in front of the post office, holding the familiar-looking envelope in his hand. Another notice of insufficient funds.

I'm too young to be in this kind of mess.

Only a few months out of college, with his first good job, Clay thought he should be living on easy street. Instead, tension and worry often crowded his thoughts.

He started on this slippery slope a few months earlier, writing checks on Thursday knowing they would not be due for payment until after his automatic deposit each Friday. Later, he began the habit of buying a few grocery items on Wednesday after church, knowing the convenience store would not make a deposit until Thursday. He had figured out that if the store used a different bank than he did, he would enjoy a day's grace before having to cover the check.

Embarrassed at his first overdraft, he thanked the bank for holding the check a few hours until his paycheck was credited. They had charged him $20.00 for the courtesy, but other than that, it had been relatively painless.

Then, the amount debited each week grew. Now, outstanding checks and overdraft charges consumed more than half of his paycheck each week. He struggled, buried in a hole he had dug himself.

In despair, he sat in his car, laid his head against the steering wheel and prayed, "Oh God, please help me. Show me the way out of this mess." When he raised his eyes and looked around to see if anyone had observed this moment of weakness, he saw the wallet lying on the ground next to the mail slot.

"Thank you, Lord!" Clay jumped out, picked up the wallet and got back in the car. Again, he checked to see if anyone had noticed. The parking lot was empty. He turned the leather billfold over in his hands, rubbing his fingers across the monogrammed *C* on the outside. He peeked inside.

Money! Lots of $20 bills. This much cash would put him on an even keel again. *Surely, surely an answer to prayer! God is so good!*

"Hey, that's not your money."

Clay looked around to see who had spoken. No one was in sight. From time to time in his life, he had heard this voice in his head, his heart, or deep in his soul nagging him about something. *"Tell the truth." "You don't need that." "Call your mother."*

His mother. She had said the voice was scriptural:

"I will put my law in their minds and write it on their hearts." (Jeremiah 31:33)

But then, she could find a Bible reference for everything that happened.

Well, maybe I can too. God helps those who help themselves.

"Except that's not in the Bible. And I said 'That's not your money.'"

Clay always found the messenger impossible to ignore, so this time he responded.

"Yes, it *is* mine. God answered a prayer. I asked for help, and he sent it."

Clay lay the wallet on the seat beside him, quickly started the motor and turned on the radio.

"What about the one who lost the billfold?"

Ignoring this comment, he turned his full attention to tuning the radio, settling on an Oldies station. The speakers blared a Christian/pop song about how God is watching us from a distance. He quickly snapped it off and pulled out into the traffic.

Parking at the bank, Clay decided to fill out the deposit slip in the car. He counted the bills and wrote "$500." on the cash line.

"I said, 'That's not your money.'"

"I heard what you said," Clay spoke aloud. "And I told you God sent it to me. I'm miserable and he wants me to be happy. He's working in my life!"

"What about the one who owns the wallet? Is God working in

his life, too?"

"Well, God's helping him give charity to a poor guy who needs it."

"Do you really believe that?"

In the middle of signing his name, Clay stopped. He did not believe that. How long would he keep fooling himself? He needed help, but this wasn't the way. God's law written on his heart would not let him continue.

Clay shook his head, trying to understand.

I asked God for help and I thought the wallet was the answer. But how can it be?

With a sigh, he opened the billfold again to look for identification. He pulled out a business card.

Martin Campbell
Christian Financial Counseling
501-555-3154
"Experience debt-free Peace"

Clay smiled as he held the card in his hand. "Yeeessss," he said softly. "Thank you, Lord. Your answer is in the wallet, after all."

~~~

One-Date Wonder

"I don't care what you say, I'm not going." Amy Ann fastened a bowtie to the collar of her tuxedo shirt and smoothed her apron.

"Why not? He's a nice guy. Really." Kerri said, as she tugged panty hose up over full hips and slipped her feet into black pumps.

The girls stood side by side in the employees' dressing room, and looked at their reflections in the full-length mirror. The two attractive twenty-somethings were uniformed and ready to serve customers at Washington, D.C.'s *Tres Bien*.

Amy Ann met Kerri her first day at work in the posh restaurant/bar frequented by a wide variety of clientele, from senators and high-ranking military personnel to famous sports figures. The girls hit it off immediately, each having her own reasons for moonlighting as a waitress. Amy worked to supplement her salary at a non-profit agency and Kerri needed extra money to help buy books, and other essentials, for grad school. Best friends for the past three years, they had supported each other through the various roller-coaster rides of meeting and dating men in a city where the odds were overwhelmingly in favor of the guys.

Kerri sprayed and scrunched the sides of her medium length hair and repeated her question. "Why not?"

"Because I don't do blind dates, that's why."

"Oh, come on, Amy Ann. You do, too. Lots."

"I know! I'm the one-date wonder. I meet someone and either he doesn't like me or I don't like him. So, starting today, no more blind dates for me."

"You're too particular. You want to be swept off your feet. There's no such person as Prince Charming."

"I'm not looking for Prince Charming. And I don't believe in love at first sight. I just want to get to know someone well enough to see if anything's there. Do you know how many losers I've had coffee with?"

"Losers need love, too."

"Spoken like a woman with a steady boyfriend."

Kerri smiled at the mention of Ron and their solid relationship. She made a fist and pointed to herself with her thumb. "That's me!" The girls' eyes met in the mirror and Kerri grew serious. "I just want the same thing for you." She turned to face her friend, and continued, "Okay, we won't call this a blind date. Mike was Ron's roommate in college. He flew in this afternoon on business. Go to dinner with us tonight so he won't be the odd man. Tomorrow you can begin your ban on blind dates."

Amy Ann sighed. She knew Kerri had put a lot of energy into finding eligible men. "Okay, as a favor to you. But then, you owe me big time."

"Thanks!" Kerri gave her a hug. "We'd better hit that time clock before Monster Man has a fit. There's a game in town and we'll be swamped tonight. The tips should be good, too."

The evening sped by as the girls rushed to take orders and carry food and drinks to the crowd of customers. Amy Ann had no time to think of the dinner date after work or to speculate on the man she would meet. Knowing up front that this was a one-time meeting took the pressure off. No need to worry about making a good impression. No agonizing over whether he would call later. No looking for a polite way to ditch him. Only the prospect of a free meal with no strings.

When the late-night crew came in, Amy Ann and Kerri hurried into the dressing room to change.

"Tell me a little more about this guy," Amy Ann said, as she stripped out of her server's uniform and stepped into the slacks and shirt she had worn to work. "And by the way, where are we going? I'm not very dressed up."

"We won't go anywhere fancy." Kerri zipped her skirt and buttoned her blouse. "His name is Mike Blanchard and he lives in Cleveland. He's tall, blonde and very good looking."

"If he's so great why doesn't he have a girl?"

"Shoot, I don't know. It's just dinner. Get over yourself, Amy Ann!"

The girls laughed as they scooted out the kitchen door into the parking lot. Amy Ann recognized Ron standing by the entrance. The looks of the man with Ron impressed her in spite of her resolve to stay aloof.

After a quick kiss for Ron, Kerri said, "Hi, Mike, this is my friend, Amy Ann."

"Hello, how are you?" he said, extending his hand.

Amy Ann took the offered hand and raised her eyes to meet his. "H-h-hello." To her surprise she found herself looking into the face of the person she was meant to be with for the rest of her life.

What's going on? This can't be happening to me. I stopped believing in fairy tales long ago. It's not possible to fall in love with one handshake. But I just did!

Amy withdrew her hand and brought it to her waist, where she held it, as though it were something precious and fragile.

He might have some habits I don't care for, and some of his mannerisms might get on my nerves at the wrong time of the month, but deep down and forever, I will love this man.

The foursome left the hotel in Ron's car. Dazed, Amy Ann listened to the small talk, acutely aware of Mike sitting beside her in the dark. She smelled his cologne, sensed his presence and knew he looked at her every time they passed a street light. This caused a small thrill, but it also kept her from glancing at him. She didn't want to risk eye contact. If their eyes met, she would melt and ooze into a puddle right there on the floor of Ron's car.

This is crazy. He lives in Cleveland! Long distance relationships never work out.

Ron and Kerri were discussing a club on the west side that served supper until midnight. Live entertainment and a dance floor added to the attraction. The conversation changed as Ron asked about Mike's flight and commented on the madness of Reagan International.

Feeling the need to join in, Amy Ann blurted, "So, Mike. You're from Cleveland?"

"For now, yes. My company's transferring me here next month.

I'm apartment hunting this weekend."

Well, things are looking up. Not long distance after all.

They rode in silence for awhile before Mike spoke again. "Tell me, Amy Ann, do you do this often? Go out on blind dates, I mean?"

Oh no! Now what do I say? Her mind raced. *Do I tell him the truth? Some men are put off by girls who blind-date a lot.* She took a deep breath. *But, if this is going anywhere, I need to be honest.*

"Well, this isn't the first blind date I've ever been on — but it's my last."

In the darkness, Mike reached over and took her hand.

"What a coincidence. Mine, too."

~~~

The Case of Produce That Went Missing

A Story of Crime and PUNishment

He felt pretty sure the rooster crowed every morning, even though it didn't always awaken him. Of course, while he slept he had no way of knowing if it crowed or not.

If a rooster crows and everyone on the farm sleeps through it, will the sun rise anyway?

David rolled over onto his back and looked at the digital clock just as 5:01 became 5:02. The timepiece had a large printout he could see without his glasses. It sat on his dresser, a habit begun the first time he was foolish enough to enroll in an 8:00 a.m. class. He couldn't reach it to push a snooze button or turn the thing off. He must get up and walk across the room to get relief from the infernal buzz.

Swinging his feet out of bed and trotting to the bathroom, David reflected that since coming to this farming community three years ago, he had never used the alarm. He had assumed he could wake and start his day at whatever hour he chose. That was before he remembered about roosters' early morning brag sessions.

After gathering the eggs, he sat down in the kitchen to enjoy his first cup of coffee of the day. He couldn't believe how much he enjoyed this life.

As a typical city kid, he had spent every summer here with Nana and Papa. In high school, when he and Carol broke up, it was here he came — to hide in the tree house he and Papa had built and cry for the loss of his first love.

Nana and Papa were proud of his accomplishments, most especially his being accepted at an Ivy League school. After Nana died during his junior year and Papa followed, David received the surprise of his life.

They had willed the farm to him. Twenty-one years old and a landowner, he knew he wanted to live and work on this farm. At the end of the semester, he left school — made his Yale break, so to speak — and came to live here permanently and to run the AAA Farm Cooperative Market out on Highway 35.

The store sold fresh produce, eggs, nuts, and even a few handcrafts from around the area. The county farmers brought their food to sell in the renovated building the Co-op acquired to house the Market. The Extension Homemakers displayed their quilts and decorated baskets for purchase and everyone pitched in to stock shelves and to work the different shifts. No one was getting rich, but during the months the store operated, they were busy. Passersby pulled off the highway and regular customers drove twenty miles from the city to buy fruits and vegetables.

The ringing phone interrupted his thoughts. Lisa McCarty's shrill voice came over the line.

"David, we need you here right away. It happened again."

Five minutes later, he steered his truck down the drive, headed to the market. Another break-in, the third this year. *I should have bought a burglar alarm from the guy who came around a few months ago.*

In this quiet community, investing in an alarm system seemed to be a waste of money. But, in a effort to be polite, David had taken the man's business card.

Phillip McCann
Sales Representative
First Alert Alarms

"I don't think we're interested, Mr. McCann. This is a pretty safe county. Are you having any luck with sales?"

"I expect to. I'm a very organized person, so I called on the businesses in alphabetical order. You actually are my first prospect."

"Well, good luck. Sorry I can't be your first sale." David felt sympathy for Mr. McCann; this was a tough territory for an alarms systems salesman.

***

David pulled into the parking lot just as John Brown, County Sheriff, arrived. Together, they approached the scene. Fruits and vegetables lay scattered in the aisles, the floor strewn with walnuts, pecans and peanuts. Only the handcraft section remained untouched by the vandalism. The sheriff took a pencil and pad out of his pocket as he and David walked around the building surveying the damage.

"This really takes the wind out of my sails," David said disgustedly.

"We sure haven't much to go on," John remarked cluelessly. "Did they get any money this time?"

"No. We never leave money in the register overnight. It's the same as the last two times. They trash the place and take only one particular kind of food."

"So what did they take?"

"Every single sweet potato in the house."

John made a note. "How many pounds would you say?"

"About 100. The bin was yam-packed."

"And they're worth about how much per pound?"

"Probably 17 cents. That's roughly a $17.00 robbery we just had."

***

The first break-in had occurred three months ago, on April 5. John said that to call the crime a break-in was a stretch, since any simpleton with a credit card could get past the doorknob lock on the entrance. The thief cleaned out the bin of plums, worth $35.00.

After that, David put a dead bolt on the front door, but the next month, on May 6, someone jimmied the latch on the back entrance and took the entire inventory of zucchini. Removing a few nails from the plywood, the robber entered through a boarded up window. Later, John Brown found the 50 pounds of zucchini in the Dumpster, squashed under some empty crates.

John theorized the break-ins were the work of a bunch of rowdy teens. The routine stayed the same: an easy entry with as little damage as possible, dump out most of the produce and take one bin of food. Never anything over the specified amount of $250.00, which would make the crime a felony.

After a long day of cleaning and restoring order to the Market

and before going to bed, David sat down to write in his journal:
"June 7...Another break-in today."

Something clicked in his brain. Jumping out of his chair, he danced around the room. He knew the identity of the thief! He also knew that the next robbery would be on July 8. That gave him a few weeks to prepare a trap.

He didn't tell anyone, not even the Sheriff, about his plans, lest the word get around and the suspect be warned. Also, he could be wrong. But, he didn't think so.

On July 4, after the fireworks display in town, David parked his pickup under a tree a half-mile away and spent the night in the market. He didn't expect anything to happen yet, but he wanted to be ready, just in case. The next three nights, he lay curled up in his sleeping bag in the back room of the store.

At 2:00 a.m. on the morning of July 8, David heard what he had been waiting for: the nails-on-chalkboard sound of studs being pulled from plywood. The thief was coming in through the same window as before.

David crouched between the green beans and black-eyed peas and waited as a shadowy figure came down the aisle toward the bin of turnip greens. David stepped out in front of him.

"The jig's up."

"The...what?" The dark figure stopped in his tracks. "Nobody says that anymore."

"Nevertheless. You're busted."

Phillip McCann turned on his heel and ran down the watermelon and cantaloupe row, with David in hot pursuit. As they rounded the corner, the salesman tripped over a basket display and made a crash landing in the middle of the okra. Unhurt, he scrambled to his feet, then, stepping on a stray okra pod, he performed a delayed axel and seemed to hang in mid-air for a moment before sitting ker-plop right in the cooler full of farm fresh eggs.

"Looks like the yolk's on you." David said, laughing as he whipped out his cell phone to call John Brown.

***

"Young man, you're going to jail," John said arrestingly.

"I have the right to remain silent," was McCann's dumb reply.

"You sure do. Meanwhile, put your hands out so I can cuff you," John remarked manically.

"You'll never make this stick," McCann said, missing the point completely.

"I'll see you in court," David put in judgmentally.

John put Phillip McCann in the back seat of the police car, being careful not to bump his head on the roof, then turned to David.

"How did you know he would come tonight?"

"The first day I met him, he told me how organized he is; he called the businesses in alphabetical order. When I realized the robberies had happened on April 5, May 6, and June 7, I knew the next try would be on July 8 and he must be the thief. He was trying to convince me to buy an alarm system."

"Well, I'll be John Brown," the sheriff said.

And David agreed.

~~~

I May be Driving The Wrong Way, But I'm Not Lost

Okay, so I'm directionally challenged. Given precise instructions, it's possible for me to get around in a fairly efficient manner. However, I follow directions literally and if told to take the first right turn, I will turn at that spot, be it a dead end street, tattoo parlor or a rally for re-instatement of go-go dancing.

All of this has led me on various adventures, though none so dangerous as the one involving my sweet little grandmother.

It all began on a Sunday morning when my phone rang at 9:00 a.m., waking me from a sound sleep. My etiquette left something to be desired.

"What?"

"Shayne?"

"Oh. *Nana.* How are you?" My grandmother cannot remember that I play in a band on Saturday nights and never get to bed before 4:00 a.m. — about the time she gets up. Her voice sounded cheery.

"I'm just fine and dandy this morning. How are you?"

"Good, Nana. It's kinda early." Wiping my hand across my face, I tried to focus.

"I wanted to catch you before you left for church." No problem, since I hadn't darkened the door of a sanctuary since the band landed this gig. "I'll just keep you a minute. Will you do me a favor?"

"Sure, anything."

"Can you go to Mrs. Scroggin's house and pick up an afghan for me? I loaned her my pattern and now I need it back."

"Sure, where?"

"On into the city a little ways; I can tell you how to get there."

"Okay, shoot." I grabbed pen and paper.

"Exit off the highway…"

"Wait, do you know which exit?"

"Well, no, but it's there where the Wal-Mart used to be."

"Nana, I don't know where Wal-Mart *used* to be."

"Yes you do. It's right there at that exit."

"Is anything else there?"

"One of those stores where you rent movies, I think."

"Blockbuster. Okay, I know where you are. Now, what's next after I exit?"

"Just go on down for a couple of blocks…"

"On the service road?"

"On that street there by that store."

"Okay, go for two blocks."

"Yes, then turn east…

"East? Let's see, …that would be right."

"…and it's in the Windtree Apartments."

"Apartments?"

"Yes, turn into the parking lot and go over three speed bumps. It's number 4-K."

"Three speed bumps…4-K. Nana?"

"Thank you, sweetie. My ride's here for Sunday School. I need to go. Thanks again."

"Nana…?" But she was gone.

My grandmother has been there for me all my life and there is no way I ever refuse any favor she asks of me. So, I hit the shower briefly, just long enough to wake myself up, and took off in my old Chevy to run this errand for Nana.

I cruised along the highway toward the inner city, looking for the exit. Sure enough, I spotted the Blockbuster just a couple of seconds too late. Leaving the Interstate at the next ramp, I turned under the overpass then doubled back to get to the service road on the right side of the highway. I think.

My notes said to travel a couple of blocks down the street in front of the Blockbuster. That would have been clear, except that the video store sat on a corner. Which street? Knowing the former location of the Wal-Mart would definitely have been helpful.

Obediently, I drove two blocks and turned right (east, maybe?). Nana hadn't said how far down that street the apartment complex was. The neighborhood looked a little seedy. I was about to give it up when I saw the sign:

Windsong Apartments
LBJ Housing Project

Nana's friend lived in the Projects? My note said "Windtree" but considering the directions Nana had given me, I decided this must be the place.

The driveway into the parking lot took a curve around the first unit. Sure enough, a speed bump lay across the path. After crossing two more bumps, I saw the letter "K" on the nearest building. And right at the end of the building was K-4. *Hey, this is my lucky day.*

I parked, got out and approached K-4 just as the door to K-3 opened.

"GET DOWN!"

Now, there are times when someone gives you a directive and you just know in your heart that you need to do as you are told — immediately — do not pass GO — do not collect $200. This was one of those times. I hit the dirt.

A volley of gunfire exploded above me. I covered my head and tried to bury myself in the asphalt. The sound of the initial shots faded away and were replaced by shouted commands to lay down guns and come out with hands up. My eyes peeked through shaking fingers as SWAT Officers' combat boots ran past me into the apartment building. Strong hands took hold of my upper arms and lifted me to my feet.

"Who are you, son, and what are you doing here?"

"I — I just came by to pick up an afghan…"

Before the last consonant left my lips, my face was pressed against the hood of the nearest car and, with the help of the policeman, the fingers of my right hand touched the back of my head.

"Hey, Bob, this guy says he's here to pick up an Afghani. We might need to call the Terrorist Squad."

My face squashed sideways and my nose practically in my mouth, I managed to say, "An *afghan*. You know, one of those blanket things little old ladies crochet."

The officer released his hold but didn't holster his gun while he questioned me further. After some time, he decided my story was true, probably because it sounded too ridiculous to be made up. He also let me know that I was in the wrong apartment complex, at the wrong end of the street on the wrong side of the Interstate.

After following a patrol car to the *Windtree* Apartments and retrieving the afghan from Mrs. Scroggins, I made my way to Nana's house. In her sunny kitchen on that Sunday afternoon, she offered me a glass of milk and warm chocolate-chip cookies.

"Thank you for picking up my afghan, honey. Did you have any trouble finding the place?"

Swallowing a big mouthful of the delicious mixture, I wiped the moustache away before answering.

"No, Nana, a nice police officer helped me."

~~~

Something About Freddy

Late one summer afternoon, Freddy lay stretched on the bank of the river near his home. The sun was shining on the clean, cool water. He closed his eyes and dozed. Suddenly a shadow fell across him and Freddy looked up, expecting to see clouds blocking the sun. Instead, he saw the beast.

All his life, Freddy had heard stories from members of his tribe who claimed to have seen creatures from another world, but it had sounded like make-believe. Freddy thought, *the stories must be true!*

He made himself lie still, hoping the alien would not be able to see him. These creatures were said to have very poor eyesight.

But, Freddy was curious about the strange being, so he sneaked a look. The alien loomed a thousand times larger than Freddy. It moved on four legs, like a mammal. It had no tail and no fur, except a short mane. The beast stood on its hind legs and stepped backward. To Freddy, this seemed like a good time to escape. If he jumped into the river, dove deep, and swam as far as possible before surfacing, he should be out of the monster's reach. With all his might, he sprang toward the water.

The monster moved — very quickly for one so large. Before Freddy hit the water, he became tangled in a trap made of webbing stronger than anything he had ever seen. He fought with all his might against the ropes. He poked one leg through a hole in the web, but the opening was not large enough for the rest of his body. The beast brought the trap close to its face and peered at Freddy. It wrapped its huge paw around his body, took him out of the snare and dropped him.

Freddy landed on his feet and moved rapidly to put distance

between him and his captor. POW! He crashed into an invisible wall.
Recovering, he sprang in the other direction only to hit the wall once
again. He lay on the hard floor, panting, trying to figure out where he
was.

The room seemed to be round and narrow, with no ceiling. *An
opening! A way to escape!* Freddy jumped, grasping at the walls,
which turned out to be slick, with no roughness to help him get a
foot-hold upward. His captor must have noticed his efforts because,
with a loud snap, a metal ceiling fell into place.

Determined he would not die or be captured without a fight, he
leapt as high as he could, again and again, trying to grab onto
something. Finally, he collapsed.

As he lay there, sadness came over him at the thought that he
would never see his family again. Only a short time ago he had been
so happy and free! He wondered if his tribe would guess what had
happened to him, since no one had seen the kidnapping.

He felt a motion that told him he was being moved to another
place. The alien was taking him away from his home.

After traveling a short time, the movement stopped. The alien
had put the cell down and removed the ceiling. Freddy tried a few
jumps, although he knew it would do no good. Through the clear
walls of his cell he could see the alien moving around. Maybe the
beast didn't plan to kill him right away.

Just then, the walls shook. The beast stood on its back legs,
towering over the prison. It roared and banged its paw against the
outer wall, making a terrible noise. Freddy trembled with fear.

The alien was joined by another of the species. This one was
larger and with a much longer mane. Its claws were tipped with red.
It roared and the smaller beast answered.

The roars must be their way of talking, Freddy thought, *they're
probably discussing me!*

Then, a third creature appeared, larger than either of the other
two, with hardly any mane at all. It pointed toward Freddy, waving
its paw and giving out a deep roar.

Oh, no, thought Freddy, *they're deciding whether to keep me as a pet
or slice me open to see how I work.*

The creature picked up the cell in its paw. Once again, the steady movement let Freddy know that he was being taken to a new place. He could not imagine what might be in store.

As he traveled, Freddy heard familiar night sounds and smelled the damp air of the river. The alien removed the ceiling door and, without warning, it reached inside the prison and scooped Freddy up in its paw.

Freddy kicked as hard as he could. He wiggled. He squirmed. *It worked!* Suddenly, he slipped through the beast's paw and dropped to the ground.

He landed on all fours and moved away quickly toward the riverbank where he had been lying earlier in the day when the creature surprised him. *I'm free! I'm going home!*

As the sun slipped behind the trees and the day ended, Freddy hurried to the quiet inlet where he made his home, hopped on a lily pad, sighed with great relief, and said,

"Ribbitt."

~~~

So Close

"I'm shaking the dust of this crummy little town off my feet and…"

Nancy Lou smiled as she quoted the famous line from the movie, *It's A Wonderful Life,* when the hero eagerly made plans to leave the small town of Bedford Falls. Boy, did she know how George Bailey felt! Her entire life had been spent in Williamstown, Arkansas, a do-nothing, know-nothing, one-horse town.

The wonder of it all is that I know as much about life as I do…and what I don't know, I'm eager to learn.

Life in a small town was happy enough for a kid. Especially a child like Nancy Lou. Her teachers loved her. Not just because her dad was principal of the High School, but because she was such a sweet person. She always remembered to say "ma'am" and "sir", even after cable came to Williamstown and kids started watching sit-coms and good manners pretty much went out of style. Also, she could always be trusted to do the right thing, tell the truth and to be completely honest.

One might think that her peers would label her a narc, as tattletales were called. But her classmates liked Nancy Lou and respected her values. They shrugged when she named the person who smoked in the bathroom.

"She couldn't help telling," they said. "The teacher *asked.* And Nancy Lou can't lie."

As she grew older, she learned to avoid volunteering information. *Don't ask, don't tell…if you don't ask, I won't have to tell.*

Childhood in Williamstown sped by, filled with play dates, Little League and birthday parties. Every summer, children went from church to church, week by week, attending Vacation Bible School, carefully planned to avoid conflicting dates. Winter brought at least one day of snow or ice when school let out and the kids rode garbage can lids down the hill behind the baseball park. A very Bedford Falls kind of existence.

Six months after Nancy Lou graduated high school, she married Ronnie Black, the boy she had been in love with since Junior High. Her dad had hoped she would go to Arkansas State, but finally had to give over. The excitement of the head cheerleader for the Williamstown Warriors marrying the captain of the football *and* the basketball teams sent everyone into a tizzy. Showers and parties honoring the happy couple swamped *CHARLA'S GIFTS AND MORE* with special orders. Weekly trips to the strip mall in Spring City became routine, as the wedding date neared.

Preparations for the nuptials the week before Thanksgiving in the sanctuary of the First United Methodist Church, kept Nancy Lou's mother beside herself. The dress, from an exclusive shop in Little Rock, was the talk of the town. Discussions of the professionally designed wedding gown (in Williamstown, for heaven's sake, where most girls wore clothes made by mothers, grandmothers or aunts) dominated the conversations at Jennie's Styling Salon.

The ceremony went off without a hitch. An absolutely perfect event…except for one thing. Ronnie not only refused to wear a tuxedo but didn't want anyone in his party to wear one, either.

"I'm not driving twenty miles to Spring City and spending fifty bucks to rent a monkey suit I don't want to wear in the first place. My Sunday clothes will have to do," Ronnie told Nancy Lou the week before the wedding. Then, without thinking, he said, "That'll be okay, won't it?"

If he expected Nancy Lou to lie for the sake of keeping down an argument or saving his feelings he simply was not thinking clearly. She informed him in no uncertain terms that it was not okay. Her parents wanted her to have the best wedding possible. They were prepared to spend all her college fund, yet Ronnie balked at fifty dollars. A huge fight followed.

They kissed and made up the next day, both learning a valuable lesson in the process. For Ronnie: don't ask Nancy Lou a question unless you want a clear, honest answer. She is not able to tell even the whitest fib. For Nancy Lou, the incident reinforced her resolve to avoid at all costs being put in a situation where she had to tell an unpleasant truth.

After their honeymoon to Nashville, the newlyweds returned to Williamstown. Promoted to full-time manager of one of his dad's mini-storage units, Ronnie and his bride would live in the small apartment behind the office.

Nancy Lou loved decorating their new home and, in no time, the living room/bedroom and kitchen/dining areas featured as many wedding presents as possible. Some of the fancier gifts, sterling silver candlesnuffers and crystal wineglasses, were stored in Unit 23 for the time being. At least until they had a place of their own. She took a job at the video store in Spring City to help build up a savings account.

So, five years later, she stood in the same apartment she had been carried into as a bride. *I'm twenty-three years old and in a rut. Life in a small town may be great for kids, but for grown-ups, it stinks!*

Standing at the dresser, she dumped her make-up tray into a large purse, reached into the drawer and put clean panties and bra in the side pocket.

This is enough. Everything else I need, I'll buy new. If Ronnie looks in here he won't miss anything.

Her plan was perfect. Leave as though she were going to work in Spring City, then stop down the way and call in sick. Ronnie wouldn't miss her until late in the afternoon when she didn't return home. By then, she would be long gone.

She'd take half the balance of the savings account. Only what rightfully belonged to her.

However, she couldn't go to the bank and risk questions from Mrs. Bullard, the main teller, who rented Unit 42 to store some family items last year when her Mama passed away.

I'll stop at the U-Totem out on the highway, call in sick and use the ATM to get the money.

She threw the heavy purse into their Camry and walked into Ronnie's office. She had hoped he might have a customer or be on the telephone, so she could blow him a kiss and leave. But, no.

"Hey, Babe." His face lit up as she walked through the door.

"Hi and bye. I really need to go." They kissed and she turned away, fearing what Ronnie's next words might be.

"Be careful. What you got planned for supper?"

"I really haven't thought that far." (Nancy Lou answered honestly.)

"Mama and them says to come over."

"Okay. Bye."

Nancy Lou scooted out the door and slipped under the steering wheel. *Whew! That was close!*

If Ronnie had asked her pointedly about her plans for today, she would have told him. And, if he knew, he would try to talk her out of leaving and create a big scene. No, this was best. Let it dawn on him gradually. When he couldn't stop her.

She drove east on Main Street past the bank, the City Café, the car wash. As she passed the corner of 4th and Main, Jerry Brown waved as he entered the lot of Brown's Best Used Cars. Once again, she thought of George Bailey running through downtown Bedford Falls, greeting the familiar business places.

Goodbye, Williamstown. It was okay for awhile, but now I'm outta here.

She stopped at the intersection of Main and Center Street. Driving straight on Main took her to Highway 14, to Spring City and the video store. Center Street led to US 65, to Little Rock, and beyond. She turned right, onto Center.

Up ahead, she saw the town's lone traffic light turn green.

Green for go. When I make it through that light, I'll be free. She sped up slightly, passing the Shell station. The light flashed yellow.

No! I can't wait even 60 seconds to be rid of this place. She jammed the accelerator to the floor, determined to cross the street before the light turned red.

* * * *

"Nancy Lou?" She tried to open her eyes, but the room was too bright.

"Nancy Lou?" Through slits in her eyelids she saw her husband beside the bed. Ronnie took her hand. He held it to his face and exhaled a shudder.

"Oh, Babe, thank God." She turned her head away. Tears fell on the stenciled pillowcase.

"Don't cry, Babe. You're gonna be okay." He pulled tissues from the box on the bedside table and gently dabbed at her eyes.

"You must've been squeezing the yellow light and that pick-up rushed the green. You're really lucky. The car is totaled." He tossed the tissues into the wastebasket.

"Just one thing I don't understand, Nancy Lou." He lowered the bed rail and laid his head on the pillow next to hers. "What were you doing over on Center Street, anyway?"

Then it all poured out. The more she revealed her discontent with their life, the more she cried and the tighter Ronnie held her, occasionally interjecting "It's okay, Babe. It'll be okay." By the time her sobs subsided, Ronnie sat in the middle of the hospital bed holding Nancy Lou in his lap.

"Oh, Ronnie," she hiccupped, "I really love you. But I'm so bored!"

"Okay. Okay, okay. We'll fix it. Do you want to go to school? Have a baby? Buy a house?" He hesitated. "Maybe you need to talk to someone about how you feel."

She winced a little at the small town euphemism for counseling, all the while realizing the suggestion made more sense than anything else he'd said.

"But whatever we do," Ronnie went on, "Every day I'm gonna ask you how you are."

And they both knew that was the best idea yet. Because, after all, Nancy Lou couldn't lie.

~~~

The Contract

Does God forgive broken promises?

Angie pondered this thought as her finger idly traced the scar on her wrist. Will God understand that sometimes we say we'll do something and when the time comes we just can't?

Of course, Dr. B. took issue with the word "can't." She always said, "Maybe you can't sing. You probably can't fly. But, you can pick up a phone."

"That is true," Angie said aloud. The bathtub full of water gave her voice resonance. "I can make the call. But, I don't want to. I'm afraid of interference."

She couldn't take a chance on someone stopping her. Gail was gone this weekend. Angie should do it while she had the place to herself.

Earlier today, when she picked up the mail, the official envelope from the State Pardon and Parole Board caught her eye immediately. She stared at the unopened letter lying among the stack of Christmas cards. She knew what it said.

"The offender in your case will be reviewed for parole...you have the right to appear...make a statement..."

He's up for parole and I'm still in prison.

Holding the envelope, she climbed out the window onto the fire escape, three stories above the street. She sucked the cold air into her lungs, hoping to clear her mind. Her thin jacket gave little protection from the icy wind as she leaned against the frozen wrought iron banister that framed the landing. Removing the letter from the envelope, she tore it in half...and half again... and again, as many times as she could. Opening her hand, she watched the bits of white paper float away in the frigid updraft of the alley beside the building.

Dr. B. says it's time I took charge of my own life. If I want closure, it's up to me to do something about it. By the time she reentered the warmth of the apartment, she had formulated a plan.

Gail left on a ski trip right after work and then Angie decorated the little tree. She hung lights and a few ornaments on its scrawny branches and topped it off with the homemade aluminum foil star. The radio provided music of the season while she addressed her few cards, adding personal notes to some of them.

These preparations finished, she soaked herself in deep, luxurious foam. Bubble baths were a nightly ritual. They soothed, comforted and calmed her frayed emotions.

She pulled the plug and stepped out onto the mat. It felt sticky with hair spray, so she quickly found her slippers, toweled herself dry and put on her robe. The last of the water drained away; scented foam lay in a heap under the perpetual drip of the faucet.

For a moment, the gaunt face looking back from the mirror startled her. The puffy dark eyes witnessed to nights without sleep. She opened the medicine cabinet and the image went away.

Well, I've been soothed by bubbles, now I will calmly take about twenty sleeping pills.

She lifted the bottle from the shelf and walked through the apartment she shared with her cousin. After Angie lost her job, Gail had taken her in. During the months that followed, when Angie could not work, Gail had been supportive, encouraging her to seek counseling. Every little bit of progress she had made, Gail had been right there with her.

She'll be glad for this to be over, too.

Seated at the kitchen table, Angie dumped out the capsules. She meticulously placed them in a neat row, the red end on top, the yellow on bottom. She rearranged them, lined them up end to end, alternated colors, made checkerboard designs.

"Let's see," she said aloud, "Do I want to chase them with water or something a bit stronger?" Vodka would be more lethal, if she could keep it down. But, if she threw up...

Water, then. She got a bottle of Aquafina from the fridge.

Everything ready, she thought again of The Promise. How many people had she made that contract with anyway? Dr. B., Gail, the nurse in the E.R., the counselor on the crisis line... Every euphemistic phrase possible had been used: when you're depressed, feel alone, think you can't go on, want to hurt yourself, yada, yada, yada. But they all meant the same thing. Before you pull that trigger, take those pills, jump off a bridge or slash your wrists...promise me, before you commit suicide, you will talk it over with someone.

If I tell them, they'll send me to the hospital. Or, at the very least, insist on another contract. I suppose I could take all the pills and then phone. But I agreed to call before.

She dialed the number on the card taped to the telephone and held the receiver to her ear. As the first ring ended, panic gripped her. She slammed the phone down before anyone could answer.

No! I'm not ready! I don't want to talk about it. Promise be damned!

A flashing memory of the rape came to her. One terrible night that changed the course of her life. She should have locked the car. Even those few minutes while she paid for gas. Enough time for him to slip into the back seat.

The volunteer who came to the hospital gave her Dr. B.'s card. But, she didn't see the doctor right away. Not until Mark left, saying she needed to "lighten up." Not until her boss told her to take a leave of absence and pull herself together. Not until Gail found her lying in the bathroom, her wrists bleeding from the razor cut.

Once more, she touched the scar. Was the rape her fault? Or God's cruel punishment for her carelessness? Months of counseling. Still looking for answers.

Then, the trial. She had to tell — relive — everything he did. Trembling in the witness chair, while the man who brutalized her sat at a table ten feet away, she listened numbly while the defense attorney attacked her character.

Since that time, she had faced squarely the question of whether she had the right to take her own life. She believed God wanted her to live in the best way she could... but she also believed God gave her the right to end this existence when it no longer had purpose and value.

She made the arrangements in a responsible manner. Gail would find her, but the scene would not be too horrible. Nothing like before.

Dr. B. often said that Angie had come a long way in the journey toward healing. That each step she took...steeled herself to take...brought the whole incident that much closer to being over.

But, it will never be over. He got 15 years. My sentence is for life.

She stood. The room tilted, then rocked. Her heart pounded in her ears. With every beat, the pain in her chest grew sharper. She gasped, lowered herself to the floor and curled up in a fetal position. The loose robe fell open, exposing the thin body to the stark overhead light. With eyes closed tightly, she concentrated on breathing slowly, deliberately. Inhale-two-three-four; exhale-two-three-four.

After a few minutes, her breath came normally and her pulse slowed. She became aware of her surroundings: the cold linoleum, the soft whir of the electric clock, the blinking of the Christmas lights in the next room. She lay there, experiencing a strange feeling of accomplishment at having managed the episode alone. Dr. B. would say, "I'm proud of you. You're very brave."

But, seeing Dr. B. again wasn't part of the plan. And Angie did not feel brave.

Facing a panic attack takes courage, I suppose. She sat up and wiped her face on the end of her robe. And it will take guts to swallow a handful of pills and fall asleep, knowing I'll never wake up. So, which is braver? To live with the pain — or to die and stand before God with a broken promise on my soul?

She pulled herself into the chair and took a long drink from the bottle of water on the table. To die or to live.

Her finger touched the redial button. A voice interrupted the second ring, "Crisis Line, may I help you" Angie took a deep breath.

"Yes — I — promised I would call."

~~~

In Our Seventeenth Summer

Art closed the trunk of his mother's 1949 Ford and picked up an armload of blankets. Following Penny down the path to the boat dock, he watched her ponytail bounce as she walked. He loved her ponytail. When she pulled back the mass of pale blond hair, little curls escaped and formed a soft halo around her face.

Penny's best friend, Elaine, started dating John right before the end of school and the four became inseparable. John's car ran most of the time, so the group had wheels to depend on when Art couldn't use his mom's car. They double-dated for all the school activities: Spring Fling, Senior Banquet and Graduation for Art and John. Three weeks into the summer of 1955 and they were having a blast.

On this particular day, John had made arrangements to borrow a boat so they could row to a small island for a picnic. They tried for an early start but the hot Texas sun was mid-high by the time they arrived at the lake.

"Gosh, looks more like a two-man boat to me." John frowned as he put the picnic basket on the ground. "Maybe it won't even hold four people."

"Come on," Penny said. "Elaine and I have been fixing food since dawn. We're not about to cancel now."

"Yeah, John. I hate to disappoint the girls. It doesn't look so bad." Art reached into the stern and picked up a small round life preserver and held it over his head. "This will save us!"

The girls laughed and Elaine said, "Let's get with it!" The boat rocked slightly as she put the basket of food into the bow.

***

Everyone thought Art Jansen and Penny Pennington were the

cutest couple in Denison High School. Even I thought so, and I was in love with Art Jansen.

We met at play practice when we each had a part in the school production of *Oklahoma*. He offered a ride to the first read-through and I agreed. We had great fun and when Art kissed me good night, I fell completely in love. That kiss! Art leaned down slightly — he was just the right height — touched my face with his fingers and kissed me on my mouth, his lips slightly parted.

In the Fifties, most kids engaged in closed-mouth kissing. The movies, our school of lovemaking, taught us that technique. We watched the professionals to master the art. Slumber parties or locker rooms provided opportunities for discussion groups. We tested our learning on our front porch swings or in parked cars. According to the slumber party talk, horn players were the best kissers. Art played the French horn, which made him the maximum utmost. I melted right down to my penny loafers.

Between scenes at rehearsals, Art and I talked and laughed together easily. We discussed current events, cheerleader tryouts and State Band competitions. We confided our long-range goals. Art planned to join the Air Force after graduation. A four-year stint in the service would earn him money for college, where he wanted to study engineering. Like most girls I knew, I was set for life: go to work for my Dad, marry some day and raise a family right there in Denison. How could I know the events of that summer would change all that?

After the play, Art stopped asking me out. No argument, no break up. To Art, we were friends who had dated for a while. He didn't know I was in love.

That wouldn't have mattered anyway, after he met Penny. She transferred late in the first semester and Art fell for her right there in chorus class with all of us watching. Every day he walked her to class, the palm of his hand touching the small of her back, guiding her through the halls. They looked *good* together. They were a perfect couple in all the ways that were important in a small Texas town in the Fifties. After they started dating, Art forsook his pompadour for a crew cut and he looked so good it made my heart hurt.

Penny's family attended a Freewill Baptist Church. She didn't dance, which was a major part of any get together in Denison, but Art never cared for dancing anyway. Their dates consisted of movies, church activities and family outings. The Penningtons embraced Art and included him in their gatherings. Each time the couple left on a date, Mr. Pennington punched Art on the arm and said, "You take care of our little girl, Mister."

That was a Fifties' thing. Boys should be responsible, take care of the girls they dated. Drive safely; don't take her places she shouldn't go; don't touch her inappropriately. Art took this charge seriously. He loved Penny and wanted to be with her the rest of his life.

When summer came, they made a familiar sight dragging Main Street with Elaine and John in Mrs. Jansen's Ford or John's old ragtop. The four spent most of their free time at Lake Texoma. This lake came into being when the Denison Dam was built across Red River where it forms the border between Texas and Oklahoma. The area sported several beaches, though there were also many treacherous spots where deep holes, trees and brush made swimming dangerous. Each year, stories circulated about someone who waded in and disappeared, only to be found later in a 50-foot drop-off entangled in brush. So, they all knew it was not safe to swim in that part of the lake. And they hadn't planned to. But what else could they do?

***

The four teens climbed in and pushed off from shore. About thirty feet from the bank, the lake became a bit choppy and Art took his first serious look at the craft they were in.

"Hey, we're riding pretty low. I think we need to go back."

The others nodded agreement. John reversed his oar in an effort to turn. Art did the same, making their efforts futile. The boat rocked and became unsteady.

"Art?"

"Don't worry, Penny. John, *pull!*" Water sloshed around their shoes as the two boys strained every muscle. The boat came around parallel to the land, rocking dangerously.

"We're going over!" Art shouted as they suddenly took on water. "Hang onto the boat! It'll float upside down."

They slid into the lake. Their clothes, heavy with water, almost pulled them under. The boat finally settled bottom-side-up as the lone life preserver floated off in its wake. Four gasping teenagers clung to the side of the upturned craft.

"We can't hang here all day, we're gonna have to swim for it." Penny spoke through clinched teeth. Her voice shook.

"Let's paddle for the bank. We can push the boat in front of us," John said, moving into position beside Elaine.

"That won't work!" They heard the panic. Penny pushed off and started to swim toward shore.

"No! Penny! Come back!" Their voices resonated across the water.

Penny took a few strokes, paused and sank below the surface. Kicking with all his strength, Art pumped toward her. He could not swim in his jeans. The weight of wet denim dragged him down. Art fought with his buckle, unbuttoned his pants and kicked them off. He swam to the spot where Penny had disappeared and whipped his body into a dive.

"Oh, Penny! *Oh, no!*" Elaine, leaning her head against the rough wood, began to cry. "Elaine, I need to help Art." John's sharp voice jarred her "Take off your jeans and throw them across the bow. Hold on while we find Penny!" He wiggled out of his pants and threw them atop the upended boat, the coins from his pockets making small splashes as they fell into the lake.

"But what if something happens to you? What will I do? Why didn't Penny stay with the boat?"

"I don't know. Hold on!"

He swam to where Art was diving. They widened their circle and continued to search. Elaine peeled out of her jeans. She almost lost them but caught a belt loop just in time to keep them from sinking.

Minutes passed. Art dived with a vengeance, forcing his body deep into the chilly water, exhausting every bit of oxygen in his lungs before sputtering to the surface.

Finally, John said, "Man, we need some help."

"You go, I'm gonna keep looking."

"No! We need to stick together. Come on now, let's get some help."

"She's here somewhere. We just need to look."

"It's been too long, man. She's gone."

"She can't be." Art's voice sounded flat. But, despite his words of denial, he turned and swam back to the boat.

The three paddled for shore, reaching land near the parked car. However, the keys, in Art's pocket, rested at the bottom of the lake. Elaine and John struggled into their wet jeans; even in the midst of a crisis, John had thought to protect Elaine's modesty. Dripping wet, Art wearing only boxer shorts and a tee shirt, they hiked to the road and flagged down a motorist. Help would come, but too late. Penny was gone.

All the kids in town hung by their phones while the Rescue Squad dragged with grappling hooks for three days. Some drove out to the lake every day to watch. I couldn't do that, even if my mother had allowed it. Later, I heard that when the hook made contact with Penny's body, it snagged her in the ankle and brought her up, dangling head down. Art sat there every day. He saw them find her. He watched as the lake reluctantly released the last bit of her, that almost-white ponytail.

The high school chorus sang at the funeral. We filled the choir loft in the little church sanctuary, facing Penny's family sitting on the first pews. Art sat with them. I watched him, crying my eyes out, certain that everyone thought I wept for a lost friend. I liked Penny a lot and was sorry about what happened. Her death brought me face to face with my own mortality. But, the real reason for my tears was the raw grief in the face of the boy I loved. Art was inconsolable at Penny's funeral.

So, imagine my surprise when, a week later, he called and asked to come over. I recognized his voice with the first syllable.

"Hi, this is Art. Whatcha doing?"

"Nothing." *Well, nothing but going ape!*

"Okay…if you're not busy… can I come by?"

"What?" I understood what he said; I needed time to think. Was he asking for a date…so soon after Penny's death? What would people think?

"I said, 'can I come over.' Do you need to ask your Mother?" He was giving me a way out. I doubted the wisdom — and propriety — of seeing him, but I couldn't refuse.

"No, it's fine. Give me a half-hour." Enough time to fix my hair and run my sisters into the back yard.

In my living room, Art sat on the edge of the couch, methodically popping his knuckles. Right hand: index finger, middle finger, ring finger, pinky. Left hand: index finger, middle finger...I lay my hand on his to stop him. He stared at our hands as he spoke quietly, in short sentences.

"I just need to be around people. But folks don't want to talk about Penny. I guess they think if we don't mention her name, I'll forget. I'm not asking you for a date. I just wonder if I can come over sometimes. And sit with you...and think...and talk if I want to...about Penny...and about what happened."

He looked at me then, raising his eyebrows in question. His lips tried a smile, but his eyes were full of pain. I heard him, in my heart more than my head. He trusted me. I was a friend.

So, for the rest of the summer, Art was a regular at my house. We stayed away from the kids in town. Sometimes we played board games with my sisters. Those afternoons, we focused on having fun...far away from death and grief and guilt. Other times, we talked about hard things. He told me of the day Penny died — the bad choices that caused the tragedy. I heard every detail of the search for her body. His voice broke when he repeated Mr. Pennington's last send-off, "Take care of our little girl." And he wept at his failure to keep that charge. He had not taken care of Penny. He said he could have prevented the carelessness that caused her to die. She was a precious gift from God and now she was gone.

I remember virtually every word Art said during those remarkable weeks at the end of that summer. Often, there was nothing to say in return. I could only sit with him, hold his hand or touch his shoulder. Somehow, I knew he needed to hear that what happened was not his fault alone; it was an accident; Penny should have stayed with the boat; he did what he could to save her. We talked about God, life after death, faith and grace. We never spoke of Penny being in a "better place" because we didn't think of death that way. Until June 20, 1955, we thought North Texas was a pretty darn good place to be. We needed no better place.

And Art healed. In September of my senior year, he entered the Air Force as planned. After the wound of losing Penny became a manageable scar, he returned to the path he had chosen for his future. But my life had changed.

I did not go to work for my dad. First, there was college and then graduate school. I put in my time as an intern, enhanced my skills with clinic work and, with my brand new Ph.D., entered private practice. Hundreds of therapy sessions. Scores of clients with stories of pain and loss. Yet, often I think of the first person I walked with through the grief process. Years ago, in my seventeenth summer, when I held the boy I loved and let him cry for Penny Pennington.

~~~

The Right Question

What does Emily Post say about canceling a wedding? Tell the ushers to send the guests away as they arrive? Or make an announcement to a church full of people?

Annie gazed into the mirror and pulled a tendril of hair that Mr. Andre had carefully arranged. Her black curls set off the white lace cap she had chosen to wear with the dress ordered months ago from Wedding Creations in New York City.

Guests are arriving. The photographer has taken pictures of our parents and attendants. All is ready. Now, I need to decide if I'm going through with this or not.

Soon, Kathy, her maid of honor, would return from the errand Annie had invented so she could have time to think. She needed perspective. Should she go ahead with the ceremony and sort things out later? That would solve the embarrassment of the moment. But, is that any way to start a life together, with unanswered questions?

She applied a make-up brush to a shiny spot on her forehead and added blush to her cheeks. The sound of the organ playing the first strains of a classic melody drifted in from the floor above, the signal for her brothers to seat the guests. Her mother was putting the finishing touches on Cameron's flower basket.

Annie frowned at the thought of her daughter. The five-year-old disliked Jeff, but surely that was jealousy. That was understandable for a young child, suddenly having to share her mommy with someone new.

Annie had met Jeff a year ago when he was volunteering at Cameron's school. They struck up a conversation about a concert each had attended and the attraction grew from there. She had noticed how kind and attentive he was and how well he related to the children, especially those kids from single-parent families.

At first, Cameron took to Jeff, and he reciprocated, taking her on outings and buying her special toys. But, as Annie and Jeff became closer, the child's hostility grew, until it became impossible for the three of them to do anything together. Annie's mother said Cameron was spoiled and would get over it when Jeff became a permanent fixture in her life.

In every other way, the relationship was perfect. Annie could not believe she had found someone so caring and supportive. There had never been so much as a minor disagreement between them. Jeff brushed away every question or concern with a reasonable explanation... and a kiss.

Even that Internet thing. When the porn site popped up on her computer screen as previously visited, Annie was shocked. She knew she had never been such a place, so she asked Jeff about it. He was the only other person to use her computer. He readily explained. While trying to pull up a web site he needed, he made a typo. No one could be more surprised than he, when that picture appeared. They had laughed at what a difference one letter could make.

Annie thought back, remembering the night it must have happened. Jeff stayed over and, as she was putting Cameron to bed, he said he needed to check his email. Yes, that had to be the time he used her PC.

In the mirror, she saw the color rise in her cheeks. Was that the night? When he awakened her, eager to make love? She had been surprised at how passionate, rough, almost brutal, he had been. She blushed deeper at the thought.

At breakfast the next morning, Jeff had told her with a tender kiss that the sight of her sleeping, all tousled and vulnerable-looking, aroused his "baser instincts."

"I'm sorry if I frightened you. It's just that I love you so much."

After years of being alone, the thought of someone consumed with love for her gave Annie all the assurance she needed. Until last night. Right after the rehearsal dinner, Kathy came to her with a story that was circulating.

"I thought you should know what people are saying," she said. "Last year, a 10-year-old girl accused Jeff of touching her, calling her on the phone and making suggestive comments to her."

"That can't be true." Annie answered almost before Kathy finished. But on second thought, she recognized that Kathy had been her best friend since high school. She didn't gossip. In fact, she put their friendship on the line to do what she thought best for Annie.

Though it was late, Annie called Jeff. He insisted they meet to talk it through. Of course, he had a logical explanation. The girl played on his soccer team. Jeff called her house to ask her mother's advice about a gift for his sister. He teased the child, yes, and he was sorry she took it the wrong way. As her coach, he gave her hugs for encouragement and congratulations, nothing else.

As usual, Jeff's logic had a calming effect on Annie. They kissed and he held her as they talked. She felt safe with him. How could she doubt the kind of person she knew him to be?

"It is just so hard to comprehend," she said against his shirt, "Why that poor little girl would make up a story like that."

Jeff moved her away from him. He gripped her shoulders, his eyes blazing.

"Don't say you believe her!" He sounded angry. "She is just a kid. Who believes a kid?"

Immediately, he was calm again. He took her in his arms and his voice broke as he said into her hair, "Come on, Annie, this just has to be okay."

Now, sitting in the bride's room at the church, her friends and family gathering upstairs, she realized it was at that moment she first thought of canceling her wedding.

"Who believes a kid?" She'd heard those exact words before. But, where? When?

Oh, yes. How old was she...six or seven?

Uncle Joe had taken all the kids on a nature walk. Everyone said how Joe loved children...what a pity he had none of his own. He led them away from the others at the picnic. Then he taught them the Touching Game. He called it a secret game. They all played until one little girl began to cry. Joe scolded her, calling her a baby. He said something terrible would happen if anyone told their secret. Then, he laughed.

"Even if you tell, no one will believe you. Who believes a kid?"

In spite of Uncle Joe's warning, Annie had tried to tell. A week or so after the picnic, she said to her mother, "I don't like Uncle Joe."

"Of course you do. Uncle Joe is a kind man who loves children. He's our blood relative and I don't ever want to hear you say you don't like one of your own kin."

So, Annie didn't speak of it again. Uncle Joe never appeared at another reunion and Annie didn't hear his name mentioned in family conversations. She had no idea why. Maybe one of the other children told. Maybe someone's mother listened. Gradually, Annie forgot the incident. Until Jeff's words triggered the memory.

Annie stared into the mirror with horror. What had she said to Cameron when the child told her she didn't like Jeff? Was her daughter wanting to tell her more — needing her to ask the right question: Why? Why doesn't Cameron like Jeff?

Annie stood up. She pulled the cap from her head. Bits of stephanotis and lace fell to the floor as she yanked pins out of the Mr. Andre hairdo and shook her curls loose. The satin train dragging behind her, she strode up the stairs to the sanctuary to speak to her guests and find Cameron, pausing only long enough to slam the bridal cap into the nearest trash can.

~~~

The Dance

"And tonight…on our stage," Ed Sullivan paused dramatically, "The Bolshoi Ballet!"

I leaned forward to see the television screen more clearly. For hours, I had watched the retrospective of variety shows, hoping for a glimpse of this *Toast of the Town* episode.

The grainy quality of the kinescope made the small figures hard to identify, but I knew where to focus my attention. Ah, yes, there I stood, third from the left, poised and ready to begin.

The first strains of *Waltz of the Flowers* sounded and we swirled across the stage, executing the moves flawlessly. Most of us had entered the Soviet Academy of the Arts at age ten to prepare for Bolshoi, the world famous ballet company. The music swelled as I, Sintija Tolev, nineteen years old, performed on American television.

Mesmerized, I sat in my rocking chair, anticipating each leap and turn, remembering every detail of the choreography. My body, that had not accomplished a pirouette for ten years, and my toes, that had not been on pointe for even longer, knew exactly what needed to happen with each move. Had my flesh and bones been able, I could have danced Tchaikowsky's famous waltz perfectly.

The audience erupted in applause at the final bow and Ed Sullivan said, "We will be back in a few minutes with…" I muted the sound, caring nothing about the advertisement that followed.

I settled in the chair and closed my eyes. My heart pounded with the excitement of that evening forty years ago. The young Sintija had danced as though this were her last performance. As well it might have been.

After the curtain closed separating the ballerinas from the studio audience, we rose and quickly made our way off the stage and downstairs. Madam Nikov whispered a crisp "No talking," although no girlish chatter erupted as we scurried down a hall to meet an American dignitary. We were well schooled on the proprieties of international visits. And my mother had coached me on what I needed to do if such an opportunity arose.

With the remote control still lying in my lap, grief welled up inside me, at the thought of my mother. Though I have not seen her since the morning our troupe boarded the plane for the United States, the pain is as fresh as yesterday. My only comfort is the knowledge that I fulfilled her wish. I escaped. She could not.

When I came into her room that last day to say goodbye, my mother lay white and gaunt on the chaise. Tuberculosis had drained her strength until the vibrant, active person I loved was gone. Only her sweet spirit remained.

"Sintija, darling girl, come sit beside me." She managed to raise her arms in welcome.

I obeyed and kissed her delicate cheek.

"Tomorrow you will go to America. Have you learned the words I gave you?"

"Yes, Mama."

"Then, watch carefully for your chance. Do not fail. It is what I want most for you."

As the daughter of a former ambassador, Mama knew about diplomatic affairs. After Papa, an official in the USSR government, met with an "unfortunate accident," Mama conceived her plan. She taught me four simple English words I must say at precisely the right time.

Each Sunday night after the television show, Ed Sullivan invited prominent persons from the audience to come backstage and meet the performers. Providentially, an under-Secretary of the Interior attended the Bolshoi appearance…the opportunity for which my mother had hoped.

As the dignitary walked through the room, smiling and shaking each hand, I stood waiting, hardly breathing. If my plan failed, I would be sent back to Russia, never to leave again…perhaps never to dance again. The Dance had been my life since childhood. To risk that, even for freedom, was a difficult choice.

The official stood in front of me, offering his hand. I lay mine in his, met his eyes directly and repeated the words my mother had taught me, "I want to stay." I knew I had not pronounced the words perfectly, as my teeth touched my bottom lip, making a **v** sound out of the English **w**. But, he understood me.

The reception room suddenly became a flurry of activity. The man whisked me away to a private office and summoned an interpreter, Nickolai Binet. Such a kind young man, Nickolai helped me with the questions that followed. Neither the indignation of the ballet director nor Madam Nikov's carrying on accomplished anything toward having me returned to the company. The next morning, Madam sent me a cold note informing me my mother had died. I found myself alone in a strange country, seeking refuge.

It seems asylum is not granted automatically in these instances, as my mother and I had naively assumed. There must be good reason. Finally, because of the political assassination of my father, investigators determined it would be dangerous for me to return to the USSR. The United States Government allowed me to remain in this country.

Without the help of Nickolai, I could never have managed the months of red tape. We became good friends before we fell deeply in love. He is still my strength.

The Dance did not end when I left Bolshoi, as I had feared it might. I became prima ballerina in a company that traveled to small cities, staging productions in high school auditoriums for children and adults who had never experienced the ballet.

Then, the day after my forty-fifth birthday, my ankle broke. My bones began to weaken and crumble. Osteoporosis ended The Dance.

Or so I thought, until the evening I sat watching the young Sintija perform on television and my spirit danced with her. My heart did what my body could not. A dance in the heart can be danced again and again.

The Dance will never end.

~~~

Essays

Never Leave Home Without One

After potty training, reading is the best thing I ever learned.

This skill came easy to me. I remember sitting in a circle bored to tears while some poor kid struggled with "See Spot run. Run, Spot, run." I felt little compassion for the one who seemed unable to retain the word "run" from one sentence to the next.

Miss Edwina Doty, my first grade teacher, receives credit for teaching me to read. In her class, scanning ahead was a serious infraction. If she caught me turning a couple of pages to see if Spot did indeed obey his master and run, she would call my name. Oh, the humiliation of having to admit I had lost the place in *Fun With Dick and Jane!*

Mastering the ability to translate writing opened countless doors. From that point on, boredom was unknown. Sunday afternoons flew by, spent in the Alps with Heidi or solving a mystery with Nancy Drew. In second grade, I became the proud bearer of a card from the Cooke County Library in Gainesville, Texas. Before a long automobile trip, I checked out the maximum number of books allowed. If I consumed them before the ride ended, word games and Burma Shave signs entertained.

Reaching the third or fourth grade level made me eligible for a special treat. I could read to my grandfather. Papa lost his eyesight at the age of 65. He liked to keep abreast of the local news and enjoyed the *Reader's Digest* for its variety of stories from around the world. So, every evening, different family members volunteered to bring the written word to him. At last, my turn had come.

I sat on the footstool in front of his chair, the daily newspaper in hand. I read a headline to him and he determined if he wanted to hear the article. If it was a go, I dipped into the story with gusto. When I came across a word I did not know, I spelled it out. He told me how to pronounce the word and the story continued. Sometimes, while deciphering a difficult article, it might be necessary to spell out several words. Papa was a good sport about it, but I wonder how he got any sense of what I read. This regular practice served several purposes. It improved my reading-aloud skills and gave me one-on-one time with my grandparent, doing a good deed while I learned about world affairs.

Good literature from Alcott to Yerby filled my high school years. While I learned dates and political ramifications in history and civics classes, I grasped the emotional impact of the Civil War from Margaret Mitchell. The decadence of the Roaring Twenties came alive to me through the writing of F. Scott Fitzgerald. I learned how the English aristocracy lived from Daphne du Murier. The Bronte's showed me the pain of true love fraught with obstacles.

As a young housewife, books became my reward. Clean the living room and peruse one chapter. Finish the ironing and take a break for fifteen minutes. Harper Lee, Norah Lofts, Grace Metalious, and Mignon Eberhart made my world richer and wider than the scope of the small, flat Oklahoma town where I existed.

Waiting rooms provided an appropriate place and the coveted time to skim the latest novel. What? My car is ready so soon? The doctor will see me now? My motto was: A book — never leave home without one.

As I gained age, maturity and, hopefully, wisdom, I developed great compassion for the one who cannot read well enough to enjoy the excitement that comes through books. Some children still struggle, but literacy programs are now available to schools. These efforts help teachers find the best way to teach children to become successful readers. After-school tutoring and Adult Literacy programs are volunteer efforts for our family. I feel deeply for those who miss the wonder gained through the written word.

Why do I read books? Because I can. Books entertain, enlarge my world, teach me, and help me escape from the mundane.

I lose myself and I find myself between the pages of a good book.

~~~

On Lemons and Lemonade

On the last day of summer vacation, life handed me lemons. The familiar expression "*If life hands you lemons, make lemonade*" has been around for 30 years or more but has never been a favorite of mine. For a time, that phrase could be seen everywhere on posters, bumper stickers, and key chains but that's no reason to dislike it. I understand the concept of making the best of a bad situation. It's just not as simple as it sounds.   This says that if life hands me lemons, I should get some water, and then look around for some sugar – or hope life hands me some. Failing that, I must convince myself that sour lemonade is actually quite delicious. There is nothing in this platitude that allows me to complain even a little about those lousy lemons. Then, one night, a little boy taught me the wisdom of this saying.

An afternoon of shopping for clothes and school supplies with my nine-year-old son left me wanting nothing more than a bit of quiet time. Phillip and I agreed on a movie to rent and headed home, planning to spend the rest of the day in a vegetative state in front of the TV. Just as we finished unloading the car, a thunderstorm rolled in and, before it ended, the electricity went off.

Expecting the power to be restored soon, we began a Monopoly game. This activity continued until daylight faded and we could no longer tell Boardwalk from Park Place. We found candles, borrowed batteries from the remote control to put in the radio, and ate peanut butter sandwiches for supper. Phillip made paper fans for us. A round of telling ghost stories and practicing shadow puppets on the wall kept us occupied until we became sleepy. Deciding the living room was the coolest place in the house, we took to couch and sleeping bag and settled down for the night.

"Mom?" The voice coming out of the total darkness wavered a bit. Shaking off the last bits of sleep while reassuring my young son, I found the matches and re-lit the candles.

"I'm hot. What time is it?"

I looked at my watch. "3:00 a.m."

"Whoa! I've never been up this late unless I was throwing up. Can I take a shower."

Time in the tub, usually accomplished after a major confrontation, proved to be an adventure in the middle of the night.

Standing under the shower spray in the candlelit bathroom, Phillip sang and played until the water became too cold to tolerate.

He bounced into the living room full of life. I suddenly remembered that a meteor shower was expected during the night and early morning hours. At the time I read about this I had thought that, even if we were awake at that hour, we would never be able to see the meteors because of the security lights around our townhouse. Well, we were awake and there were no bright lights. So, at 4:00 a.m., on the last day of vacation, Phillip and I sat on our front stoop counting shooting stars.

The lemonade was great.

~~~

Lost

The child in the Target store suddenly missed her mother. The little girl pulled her attention away from the toy display and looked around. Her eyes grew large. She turned in a full circle, frowning, catching her breath.

I thought to speak and reassure her but, being a stranger, I hesitated. She took a tentative step down the aisle and I watched — knowing, *remembering* how she felt.

***

It was 1940. A carnival had come to town and set up in a big field at the end of Main Street. Everyone in the county must have been there. Never in all my five years had I seen such sights. Daddy bought us cotton candy and then we rode the merry-go-round. As we walked along the mid-way, I saw a man pounding a stump vigorously with a huge mallet, trying to ring a bell. The muscles across his back flexed with each swing. I stopped to watch.

He slammed a mighty blow and the "bong" could be heard all over the fairgrounds. I spun around to see the family's reaction to this amazing feat.

"Look, Mama..."

I was alone. Daddy, Mama and all four siblings had disappeared. I looked right — left — all about. They were nowhere to be seen.

My chest felt tight; I needed to go to the bathroom. My nose and eyes burned as I turned and turned, searching the crowd of strangers. What should I do? Never in my most far-fetched fantasy had it occurred to me there might be a time when Mama and Daddy were not with me. I whirled around once more.

Then, through tears, I spotted Mama coming toward me, followed by the rest of my loved ones. Saved!

Mama told me "good girl" for standing still, so she could find me by returning to the last place we'd been together. I didn't tell her I was just trying to decide which way to run.

***

The little girl in the Target store made her decision and took off in a dead heat. I followed. The mother came around the end of the next aisle, scolding the child for wandering off. I wanted to tell the mom that *she* was the one who wandered off, but again, as a stranger, I reconsidered.

The pair moved on to continue shopping, the youngster clinging to the cart. No hug, no "good girl." Maybe the mom didn't know the feeling of being lost.

But, the child will never forget.

<center>~~~</center>

Luck Is Where You Find It

One summer a few years ago, I experienced the good fortune of having a stalactite drip a bit of water on me. After a pleasant weekend in East Tennessee seeing the sights with my eight-year-old son, we climaxed our mini vacation with a visit to the Lost Sea. This huge cave with an underground lake is near Sweetwater, Tennessee, just this side of the Great Smoky Mountains.

As part of the cave tour, Phillip and I, with a group of other tourists, boated around the lake while the guide directed our attention to various points of interest. We gazed at rock formations on the lake floor that appeared to be only inches away when actually they rested in forty feet of water. As we marveled appropriately at this wonder of nature, a bit of liquid hit me on the face. I looked at Phillip as he studied the splash of water on his arm. The guide explained that the drops were from the stalactites on the ceiling of the cave. Active stalactites emit moisture from time to time. The guide assured us that this was a very fortunate happening. Stalactite drops bring seven days of good luck.

Wow! Good luck! Magic words for a child. Phillip anticipated aloud the prospect of the good fortune awaiting us during the upcoming week. For extra insurance, we rubbed the bear claw rock at the cave's exit, since that also is said to guarantee a happy future. But, as I found out later, good luck is in the eye of the beholder.

We left Sweetwater Sunday morning in plenty of time to reach Nashville by early afternoon. We planned to stop for lunch and gasoline at the halfway mark on the Cumberland Plateau. About 45 minutes from Sweetwater, where Interstate 75 merges with I-40, a truck crowded me and I found myself on the opposite end of the Y — headed in the wrong direction.

Irritated, I pulled off at the next exit into a travel-mart, deciding to fill the gas tank before making a turn-around. I pumped approximately $2.00 worth of gasoline — then suddenly realized my purse was in Sweetwater. Scrounging through the car for change and borrowing a dollar from Phillip still left me a little short, but the kind station attendant understood my predicament.

As I returned to the car and started the motor, Phillip commented he was glad we had rubbed the bear claw stone for *extra* good luck. Weren't we lucky the truck crowded us so we left the highway and stopped for gas earlier than we had planned? Because that happened, we didn't have as far to backtrack when we discovered my purse missing. And weren't we lucky that Phillip didn't spend that dollar the day before, as he had really wanted to do? While not in complete agreement with his outlook, still I was happy our luck held and a quick phone call assured me the pocket book was lying where I had left it, waiting to be retrieved.

That evening, when the same purse was snatched in the parking lot of a Nashville grocery store, Phillip's belief in our good fortune was tested again. But, when the police officer said I was *lucky* the purse was not over my shoulder (or I might have been dragged across the parking lot), and *lucky* I didn't lose my keys, and *lucky* I had only $17.00 in my wallet, and *lucky* I was able to cancel my bank card and checks right away, Phillip's confidence was restored. The next day, my purse was returned with all my ID intact and he was convinced the drip from the stalactite and the magic of the stone were responsible for things turning out so well.

Actually, Phillip's way of thinking has merit. How much better to go through life expecting the best. Maybe good things don't really come from a weeping stone, a rabbit's foot or a lucky charm. That doesn't matter. The truth is: blessings in life abound if only we recognize good luck whenever it comes our way.

~~~

When the (Potato) Chips Are Down We Do What We Must

One night, as I surfed the television channels, I happened upon an old Charlton Heston movie, *The Naked Jungle*. I stopped to watch this favorite from the 1950's. It is a story of a stiff, stern man, Mr. Heston, who built a plantation in the jungle of South America. Through years of hard work, he accomplished the near-impossible. He was proud of his farm, his house, his possessions and of himself. Then, about half way through the movie, all he owned was challenged by *marabunta* — soldier ants. Not kindly, NATO, peacekeeping soldier ants, but hostile take-over-type killers. Millions and millions of these insects marched across the country eating everything in sight: grass, trees, comical sidekicks, evil plantation owners who beat their workers — you get the picture. Charlton Heston and his beautiful lady, Eleanor Parker, survived the attack of *marabunta*, but at the cost of the plantation, which was a big mess when it was over.

Imagine my consternation the next morning when I saw, on my kitchen cabinet, thousands of ants chewing on what was once a breadcrumb. A forgotten peanut butter knife was possessed by the creatures. Ants! And me without an assault rifle! I wiped the counter, thinking that would get rid of them, only to find later that the smallest drop of food drew a crowd like Customer Service the day after Christmas. The trail went across the counter, behind the sink, up the wall and into the ceiling; the starting place was likely somewhere in Ecuador. Something must be done at once.

A local store offered a package of ant bait that declared "the food is carried back to the nest to kill the queen and destroy the entire colony." It described in detail how the poison attacked the ant's breathing apparatus, causing it to suffocate. That seemed harsh. I just wanted the ants to go away. My visual image shifted from *marabunta* to Disney characters. Was it necessary to kill the whole colony just to keep the ants out of any food that was not hermetically sealed? Must I slaughter the innocents along with the soldiers?

The answer is yes, and in the end I did it. Whether it's Charlton Heston with dynamite to blow up the dam and flood the plantation or me armed with little octagon-shaped traps to stick on the wall, we do what we must to protect our homes from the dreaded ant.

~~~

Devotionals

A Promise in Hard Times

If any of you lacks wisdom, he should pray to God, who will give it to him; because God gives generously and graciously to all. (James 1:5)

My husband and I were in our middle fifties and he had just been released from the hospital when we realized the need to provide permanent, full-time care for our four-month-old grandson. As I thought about taking on this responsibility, I prayed for some assurance that this was what God wanted us to do. So many questions loomed: Would we have what it takes to face again the stages of child rearing? Would we live long enough to do it? Was it right to intervene in this child's future? And after bringing this child into my life, would I ever be able to let him go?

Then one day in my prayer time, God spoke a message to my spirit as clearly as if I had heard an audible voice: "Whatever you need to complete this task, you will have. When you need to take action, you'll know what to do, and you'll have the ability to do it."

That was sixteen years ago. That boy has been a blessing, a chore, a joy and sometimes a headache. These years have included softball, soccer, Scouts and homework. Also, heart surgery, biopsies, retirement, and the loss of Grandpa/Daddy/husband. We felt support from a loving family and friends who helped and sustained us. Several times I have had occasion to remember the promise God gave that He will provide the wisdom, patience, finances, courage and stamina — whatever is needed — to accomplish the task he set before me.

The Upper Room - December, 1994

The Unexpected Gift

Simeon took the child in his arms and gave thanks to God. Luke 2:28

Simeon had been waiting a long time to see the Messiah. God had promised that this would happen before he died. Just knowing that he would live to experience the Redeemer establishing the Kingdom of Israel again, with power over all their enemies — well, it had kept Simeon hopeful through a lot of bad times. No doubt, he had expectations of just how the miracle would happen and what the Promised One would look like. Now a very old man, he knew that it had to happen soon because he was nearing death. Each time a bold young man spoke out in Temple, Simeon would ask, "Is it he, Lord?"

Each week, with faithful regularity, Simeon went to the Temple. This was not one of his usual days to attend, yet he felt an urgent need to go. When Mary laid the child in his arms, God must have said, "This is he, Simeon. The one I promised, the One you have waited for. It's going to be different than you expected."

Many of us, waiting for Christ to touch our lives, have expectations of how it will be — what the answer to our prayer will be — what will occur — how we will feel. We long for Christ, but could it happen we fail to recognize Him simply because He takes a form different from what we expect?

What a blessing for Simeon that he recognized the Savior in the tiny baby who was presented to him.

The Upper Room - December, 1996

Obedience

Scripture Reading: 2 Kings 5: 1-15

As I entered the computer room at work one morning, a group of co-workers stood, gathered around the laser printer.

"This printer isn't working," someone said. "We've all given it jobs, but it won't print a thing. We're calling for help."

When the word came from the Tech Support person, the instructions were, "Turn the printer off, wait two minutes, then turn it on again."

Disbelief echoed from all the employees, still hovering around the machine. "That won't work," one secretary said. "It's just too simple."

The group agreed the instructions sounded too silly to be of any use. But, lacking any other possible solution, I turned off the printer, waited two minutes and turned it on again.

Immediately, various print jobs stored in its memory began to fall into the tray.

Just that morning, I had read in 2 Kings of the healing of Naaman, a rich man who had leprosy. He traveled a long way to seek help from the prophet Elisha. When he arrived, his servant went in to Elisha to make the request. Elisha didn't even bother to see Naaman; he just sent word for him to bathe seven times in the Jordan River.

Irritated, Namaan fumed. There were rivers at home. He expected elaborate instructions, maybe even a difficult task to complete to bring about his healing. Surely not something as easy as a dip in the water.

Did I react any differently than Naaman as I struggled with a problem in my own life? I asked for God's guidance and a possible solution came to mind, but I rejected the idea because it was too simple, too easy.

As co-workers marveled at the healing of the printer, the

realization came to me: The answer is *obedience*. When I ask for help, I need to listen and follow the instructions given.

It did not matter how many times Naaman dipped in the river; the healing came because of his obedience.

And for me, it is not the complexity or simplicity of the solution, but rather my willingness to hear God's voice. Whenever, wherever or however it might come to me, I must listen and obey.

Evangel - December, 2001

Patience
(On Beans and Bulbs)

Be still before the Lord and wait patiently for him. (Psalm 37:7)

Once, when my daughter was five years old, her Sunday School teacher gave her a lily bulb. The instructions were to put it in the ground and, in several weeks, a shoot would appear and become a beautiful flower. We chose a place and Kathy planted her treasure. The next day, she ran to check on the progress. Nothing showed above the dirt so she dug up the bulb to see how it was doing. After we talked about how God makes the flowers grow, we planted it again. Later, I found Kathy spading the dirt around the spot to check the plant once more. It took several tries to convince her that her job was to plant the bulb and then *leave it alone* and give it a chance to grow. Nowadays, children in kindergarten plant beans. Beans are guaranteed to produce visible results in 24-48 hours.

We are amused at a child's impatience, but are we different? We want fast solutions to our problems, quick results from our efforts, instant answers to our prayers. We find it difficult to *leave it alone* and let God take care of it in His time.

So, before we become concerned about the status of a project, let us think: did we plant beans or bulbs? Beans grow very fast and make lots of other beans. Next year, if we want more beans, we plant beans again. Bulbs grow much slower, but they are long lasting, often returning voluntarily year after year. Both have value and there are many reasons for planting either. But we shouldn't expect bean results when we plant bulbs.

Evangel - June 2004

AWARDS

An Answer to Prayer. 2003 Honorable Mention Life Press Christian Writers Prose

Called to Be a Dad. 2003 Honorable Mention *Byline* Short Story

Consider the Bluebonnets. 2001 Third Place Fiction Writers of Arkansas Blue and Grey Contest, 2002 Editor's Choice Grandmother Earth Prose

The Contract. 2002 Honorable Mention Arkansas Writers Conference Short Story, 2002 Honorable Mention Grandmother Earth Prose

The Dance. 2004 First Place Arkansas Writers Conference Short Story

Eat Your Heart Out, Doctor Dolittle. 2001 Honorable Mention Bylines Character Sketch, 2001 Honorable Mention Arkansas Writers Conference Wit and Wisdom

Every Day a New Day. 2003 Finalist Calliope Fiction Contest, 2005 Third Place Life Press Writers Prose

How Long is Forever. 2002 Third Place Byline New Writer Contest, 2002 First Place Grand Prairie Arts Festival

I May Be Driving the Wrong Way, But I'm Not Lost. 2004 Third Place White County Creative Writers Humorous Short Story, 2005 Green Rivers Levity

In Our Seventeenth Summer. 2003 Second Place White County Creative Writers Short Story (under the title A Walk Through Grief), 2005 Third Place Calliope Fiction Contest

Lost. 2001 Third Place White County Creative Writers Conference Personal Essay

Lost and Found. 2001 Third Place White County Creative Writers Conference Short Story, 2004 Finalist Calliope Short Story

Luck Is Where You Find It. 2002 Second Place Arkansas Writers Conference Essay

Never Leave Home Without One. 2003 First Place White County Creative Writers Conference Personal Essay

Obedience. 2004 First Place Life Press Christian Writers Prose

On Lemons and Lemonade. 2004 Second Place Arkansas Writers Conference Essay

The Perfect Prize. 2001 Honorable Mention Arkansas Writers Conference Young Adult Fiction, 2003 Honorable Mention Bylines Genre Fiction, 2004 Second Place White County Creative Writers Conference Short Story

The Right Question. 2002 First Place White County Creative Writers Conference Short Story, 2003 Honorable Mention Byline Short Story

The Substitute Boy. 2005 Honorable Mention Arkansas Writers Conference Fiction

When the (Potato) Chips Are Down We Do What We Must. 2001 Honorable Mention Byline Essay

When There's Nothing To Do. 2001 Honorable Mention Arkansas Writers Conference Short Story, 2002 Third Place Grandmother Earth Prose

About the Writer

Dot Hatfield began writing at the age of nine when she received a Five-Year-Diary for Christmas. Toward the end of the Twentieth Century, she moved from journaling and company/club newsletters to writing personal essays and finally to fiction. In 2000, she retired as Coordinator of Volunteer Services at a crisis center in Nashville, Tennessee, and moved to Beebe, Arkansas, where she works as a secretary in an education cooperative.

An active member of White County Creative Writers, Dot served as President in 2005. She expresses appreciation to her two critique groups, Central Arkansas Writers and The First Monday Group.

Dot's essays, short stories and poetry have been published in *The Upper Room, Evangel, Church Educator, Calliope, Mature Living, The Reader, Grandmother Earth Anthology, Park Tales Anthology,* and local and regional newspapers.

Some of the awards she has received are from Arkansas Writers Conference, White County Creative Writers Conference, Life Press Christian Writers, Grandmother Earth, Grand Prairie Festival of Arts , *Calliope*, Green River Writers and *Byline* Magazine.

www.ingramcontent.com/pod-product-compliance
Lightning Source LLC
Chambersburg PA
CBHW020252150626
46552CB00020B/777